BY SHERRIL JAFFE

Scars Make Your Body More Interesting (1975)

This Flower Only Blooms Every Hundred Years / This Flower Only Blooms Every Hundred Years / This Flower Only Blooms Every Hundred Years / This Flower Only Blooms Every Hundred Years / This Flower Only Blooms Every Hundred Years / This Flower Only Blooms Every Hundred Years / This Flower Only Blooms Every Hundred Years / Thi

SHERRIL JAFFE
THIS FLOWER ONLY BLOOMS EVERY HUNDRED YEARS

Santa Barbara
BLACK SPARROW PRESS
1979

THIS FLOWER ONLY BLOOMS EVERY HUNDRED YEARS.
Copyright © 1979 by Sherril Jaffe.
All rights reserved. Printed in the United States of America. No part of this book may be used or reproduced in any manner whatsoever without written permission except in the case of brief quotations embodied in critical articles and reviews. For information address Black Sparrow Press, P.O. Box 3993, Santa Barbara, CA 93105.

ACKNOWLEDGEMENT

Some of these chapters, or versions of some of these chapters, have appeared, or are to appear in the following periodicals: *Credences, Eureka Review, Fiction West, Gallery Works, Gnome Baker, New Directions in Poetry and Prose, Sparrow, Wch Way.*

LIBRARY OF CONGRESS CATALOGING IN PUBLICATION DATA

Jaffe, Sherril, 1945-
   This flower only blooms every hundred years.

   I. Title.
PZ4.J215Th   [PS3560.A314]   813'.5'4   78-27461
ISBN 0-87685-417-X (paper edition)
ISBN 0-87685-418-8 (signed cloth edition)

For some things, the parts are more expensive than the whole.

For others, it's cheaper to buy the whole thing than the parts individually.

CONTENTS

Palm Springs / 11
Palm Springs Revisited / 13
Return to Palm Springs / 15
Palm Springs, as Usual / 17
Hawaii / 19
Yosemite / 25
Palm Springs Again / 29
Transcontinental Cadillac / 31
P. S. / 35
The Three and a Half Grand Tour / 37
South of the Border Between High School and College / 45
The Psychology of Sex / 59
A Modern Apartment / 63
Portland, Oregon / 69
Return to the High Country / 73
Squaw Valley / 77
Happy Valley / 91
Aspen, Colorado / 97
The Map of Happy Valley / 105
The Heart in the Bahamas / 109
Hawaiian Bargain / 113
A Wedding in the Country / 123

THIS FLOWER ONLY BLOOMS EVERY HUNDRED YEARS

Palm Springs

THEY ARE STAYING in Palm Springs where everyone wants to go. They are not actually staying *in* Palm Springs, they are staying at a motel right *before* Palm Springs. They are staying on the outskirts of Palm Springs because they got a deal on the motel. But Ann doesn't know this. She doesn't know where she is or how she got there. She probably thinks she's on a really great vacation. She probably thinks this is all there is to Palm Springs. In the center of the motel there is a pool. There are lounge chairs all around the pool. The women lie in the lounge chairs in their swim suits. Their hair is tied up in kerchiefs. Their eyes are closed under their sunglasses. Their skin is brown and greasy. Ann doesn't know how to swim. She had sat in the kiddie pool, but it was warm. And it was hot here in Palm Springs. Suddenly, Uncle Jack came up behind her sister Barbara, who didn't know how to swim, and pushed her into the big pool. That was how Barbara learned how to swim. In the other version of the story, that was how *Ann* learned how to swim.

Palm Springs Revisited

THEY ARE STAYING in Palm Springs, where everyone wants to go. They are not actually staying *in* Palm Springs, they are staying in a motel right before Palm Springs. They are staying on the outskirts of Palm Springs because they got a deal on the motel. It is a little lonely at this motel, with the desert wind blowing all around. But that is nothing to Ann. There is a pool in the center of the motel. There are lounge chairs all around the pool. Ann does not lie in the lounge chairs. She's in the pool. She's been in the pool all day. There is no reason to ever come out of the pool. The women are in the lounge chairs. Now it is growing late. Now everyone is going in. Ann is still in the pool. Now the clouds are massing overhead. Ann hopes it will rain. Then she will be swimming in the rain. It starts to rain. Ann is swimming in the rain! Now she can get reluctantly out of the pool. In one version of the story she was so fond of swimming that she stayed in the pool even though it started to rain. But in the true version of the story she had always dreamed of swimming in the rain. And so that could be said of her—she swam in the rain.

Return to Palm Springs

THEY WERE STAYING in Palm Springs, where everyone wants to stay. They were staying at the El Mirador, the best and the oldest, in fact *the* place to stay in Palm Springs. They were only staying there because they got a deal on the hotel. They were very lucky to be staying there. They really didn't deserve to stay at the hotel where Jerry Lewis stayed. But there was no way that Jerry Lewis would know this. That was why Jerry Lewis bought them cokes. He was sitting under a shade at a table by the pool playing cards, and Ann and Barbara crept closer and closer. Until he bought them cokes. But otherwise he didn't notice them. This was nothing special to Ann. Because that was the kind of thing that happened to you when you stayed at a place like the El Mirador. If you stayed at the El Mirador you didn't get excited about it.

At night, after dinner, they walked in their cotton dresses and white sweaters to the magic store. There, they were each allowed to buy one magic trick. The man in the store demonstrated the trick you picked out. He tried to fool you. Ann picked the trick with three cups. There was something the size of a pea hidden under one of the cups. The man in the store moved the cups around and around to confuse you, and you had to guess which cup the pea was under. Ann always guessed the right cup after looking for the little string which was attached to the pea which stuck out for this purpose. She always bought this trick.

Palm Springs, as Usual

THEY WERE STAYING in Palm Springs, as usual. On the way in, they had passed the little motel where they had first stayed. Ann did not admit to herself ever having noticed the place before. They passed the El Mirador. That was a good hotel, but a finer hotel had been built, since, on the other side of town. They arrived at the finer hotel. Their baggage was taken to their rooms, which were very quiet, as the hotel was so fine. The rooms were fine, they were fine people. There was no reason to get excited. Ann would have liked to get excited, but there was no reason to get excited.

After a while, they took a stroll out into the desert. The desert began just outside the hotel. There were hoof prints in the sand. If Ann had been a cowboy, she would have ridden away. But Ann knew she wasn't a cowboy. How could she be a cowboy with her parents and her sister there? Barbara and her parents turned back. Ann walked backwards in her own footprints back to the hotel, in order to leave the impression of steps taken which never return.

Hawaii

CAROL KAUFMAN'S HAIR was blond, she was tanned, and her pert nose was irresistibly peeling. She was wearing a lei of orchids round her neck. Ann watched her in the mirror of the girls' bathroom where all the girls were gathered before class. This was Ann's twelfth birthday, but Carol Kaufman was the center of attention. She was fresh off the boat from Hawaii. All these girls were kissing up to her. She didn't even notice Ann, the new girl in the mirror. Ann, who had never been to Hawaii.

The bell rang, signaling them into the classroom with the boys. There they stood by their seats and put their hands over their hearts and began the Pledge of Allegiance, one of the longest speeches in the English language. Ann was trying to remember the words when she panicked. Had she been holding her hand over her heart, or had she, by some terrible mistake, been holding her hand over one of her breasts? The heart, she knew from studying Harvey who had studied the circulation of the blood, is not on one side or the other, but right in the middle. Yet how could she put her hand right in the middle? She would look like a cripple, which might put her in an unfavorable light. And she couldn't be too careful. This was Beverly Hills. She couldn't afford to take chances. She was the new girl in the class, and she knew that how she appeared to the others in these first few weeks would determine her future position in life. She had taken the precaution of wearing her new blue paisley dress. She thought it made her boobs look big.

Such as they were. Ann looked up the row at the girl sitting in the first seat, the most popular girl in the class. Her boobs were enormous. Behind her sat the second most popular girl, with slightly smaller boobs. And behind her sat Carol Kaufman with flashing brown eyes and flowers at her breast. She had been to Hawaii on the Lurline. A place for Ann would be fixed in this line sooner or later. "Let it be beside Carol Kaufman," she prayed.

This prayer could be answered. Ann's parents could take her to Hawaii.

They weren't going on the Lurline like Carol Kaufman. They were going to fly. It was some sort of business deal Ann's father had gotten. When Ann asked Daddy which airline they were going on he told her it was a White Knuckle Flight.

Ann boarded the plane in Burbank behind a family already dressed in matching Hawaiian shirts. There *were* no more Hawaiians, the driver who picked them up at the airport in Honolulu explained. All these people were a mix-up, he said. Hawaii was a paradise of brotherly love where everybody intermarried. But if someone had really loved the Hawaiians, Ann thought, there would have been some care taken to make sure that there would still be some around. If there had, in fact, ever been any Hawaiians.

The driver had pointed out Waikiki Beach as they drove past it. There must be some mistake. Ann had thought that the Royal Hawaiian Hotel, where Carol Kaufman had stayed, was on Waikiki Beach. Ann hadn't bargained for this.

They were going to a new hotel that was the latest thing. It was bigger than the Royal Hawaiian. It wouldn't fit on Waikiki. It was bigger than one hotel. It was two hotels, plus grass shacks for honeymoons, all of the most modern design. From the window of her room on the eighth floor Ann could see the three swimming pools glimmering and the man-made lagoon far below. She wondered if Carol Kaufman had swum in a lagoon. No one was swimming in this one. Perhaps one didn't really want to swim in lagoons.

A basket of fruit arrived, compliments of the management. It was not everybody who got a basket of fruit compliments of the management. They were special guests here. It wasn't exactly that Daddy knew the owner—Henry Kaiser, a very great man—but Daddy had been of some service to him. Some little service that for some reason made Henry Kaiser think that they should not only be invited to stay at his hotel as his personal guests at a reduced rate, but that once they had gotten there they should be given special attention. Actually it wasn't Henry Kaiser himself who was making all this possible, but another man, lower down on the totem pole, whom no one had heard of, but who was important enough in his own right, whom Daddy had done the service for. Henry Kaiser didn't know anything about it. He didn't need to. He would never find them in this huge hotel, the Hawaiian Village.

That night they dined under a banyan tree. Ann was listening for the lap of the waves on the beach. "The Shirt family's here," Barbara whispered. Ann turned around to see. They had all changed into fresh identical shirts. These shirts were also of a Hawaiian pattern.

After dinner they took a stroll. The Shirt family was already strolling. They pushed past an idol and went down an arcade where everyone was coming and going past racks of Hawaiian shirts. It wasn't possible for Ann to choose among them or to decide which one Carol Kaufman might have bought because Mother wouldn't consider buying her one.

In the pineapple factory beside the Mormon Temple in the middle of the pineapple field they were giving away samples. Ann had never tasted such delicious canned pineapple. It was only afterwards that Barbara told Ann that she had made a pig of herself. She had not wanted Ann to feel bad at the time.

A pig was being lowered into a pit of hot coals and covered with dirt. It was disgusting, but it cost four dollars a person because this luau was going to be quite an experience. This poi they were being offered was very nutritious, but you wouldn't want it, the announcer said, because it tasted like wallpaper paste. "Hey, have you tried the wallpaper paste?" Daddy asked. A brown beach boy in a sarong was squatting by Mother, scooping up poi with his fingers, and sticking them in her mouth. There was a flash. In the picture, Mother looked red. Daddy paid for it.

Ann was being taken for a ride in an outrigger canoe. The beach boys did not invite her to paddle. Even if they did, she knew they would just be humoring her.

Ann was not going to make a pig of herself by asking for something to drink, she was just going to die of thirst. When she got back to the hotel she discovered something in her pants. Neither Mother nor Barbara would look. They told her she was menstruating. She thanked them for the explanation, and went along to the bathroom to figure out this Kotex they had given her. Sitting there on the toilet with the door closed she wondered if she really did have her period, or if it was some mistake.

Lunch was at a lunchroom where Robert Louis Stevenson must have lunched. He had one of the little grass shacks out back. Ann looked up from her fruit cocktail to see the Shirt family eating fruit cocktail at the table next to them.

The light was failing as they stood around in the souvenir shop trying to decide among packets of slides of Hawaiian sunsets. They were leaving for Maui on the morrow.

Maui was not a place that people usually went to, but Daddy assured them that they were lucky to be going there. Mother didn't know why they should want to go there if no one else did. Ann didn't think Carol Kaufman had gone there. She looked across the aisle of the plane at the Shirt family. The Shirt family was the most ordinary family in the world. She took Daddy's hand to let him know what a really great vacation she was having. Daddy closed his fist and extended two fingers. "Want to pet the rabbit?" he asked. There was no way to tell Daddy that she was too old to pet the rabbit. So she petted the rabbit and hated herself for not wanting the Shirt family to see.

The hotel they went to was, as Mother predicted, not very good. But there was no way Daddy could have predicted this when he had made the reservations months ago. It had never been his intention to humiliate or inconvenience his family. Ann was wearing the muu-muu she had bought at Ohrbach's a few weeks before. No one had to know she wasn't wearing a real Hawaiian muu-muu like the beautiful daughter of the King who must save her father by throwing herself into the volcano that was about to erupt.

The road up the volcano was precipitous, and the driver was driving too fast, but no one dared to ask him to slow down. Then he suddenly pulled off the road. They were not at the top. He opened the door for them, and they got out. The air was surprisingly thin.

"Here is something which you can only see growing high up on the slopes of Haleakala," the driver said, pointing to some stuff growing just beneath the road. "This flower only blooms every hundred years," the driver said. Ann looked at the two silver tufts growing in among the ordinary shrubs. She couldn't tell if they were blooming or not.

The hula dancers, wearing grass skirts, are standing in a line. Tall waving palm trees behind them. Leis of flowers around their necks. Each is holding up a huge letter. In the foreground, in the corner, is the Shirt family father's sleeve. It is blurry, but it is probably of a Hawaiian print. All together the letters spell out ALOHA. The slide show was over. Barbara pushed the light button and they were sitting in the family room. The fan of the machine was still going. The phone was ringing.

"It's Carol Kaufman, for Ann."

She was inviting Ann to sleep over. They had been together all day, sinking into the deep water of Carol Kaufman's pool, stretching out in the sun on the smooth tile. Carol Kaufman lying on the diving board, her chin to the sun.

Indeed, Ann had been with Carol Kaufman almost constantly since she had returned from Hawaii. She had run into her at Ellen's birthday party when her orchid lei was still fresh. Ann had struck up a conversation, saying how boring it was to be back in Beverly Hills after Hawaii. Carol Kaufman had agreed. "Didn't you just love the bathtubs in the Royal Hawaiian?" she had said with a lazy smile. "I never got out of mine," Ann had replied, holding her breath. "Oh, I'm so bored," Carol Kaufman had said. "Come and sleep over tomorrow night."

Now they were in Carol Kaufman's wing of the house. Her parents were asleep far away. Carol Kaufman was running the water in the tub. Then she poured a capful of emerald green pine scented oil under the tap. The two girls lay back in the tub. It was the most luxurious concoction in the world.

When the hot water at last ran out, they left the water in the tub, and squatting wrapped in a towel, Carol Kaufman reached behind the set of encyclopedias and pulled out the *True* magazine. Ann was waiting in the big bed. Then Carol Kaufman crawled in with her and started to read her the true story of a girl whose parents were dead, and she had to go and live in the house of her Uncle Jack. Her uncle was very nice to her, and his house was in the middle of a coconut grove, but there was something about her uncle she didn't like. Her uncle was always asking her to sit on his lap, and she felt embarrassed, because she knew she was too big for it. Her uncle was always trying to kiss her on the mouth and pat her sweet little bottom. She was afraid of her uncle, she couldn't escape him, he was so big, she ran to her room, the door wouldn't lock, she was lying in her bed terrified as she heard his powerful footsteps coming down the hall—"This time, you be the uncle," Carol Kaufman said.

Yosemite

THE POOL was icy cold and crystal clear. Only brave spirits could swim here. Barbara hadn't come. She was back at the hotel with their parents. Ann dove in. She was the only girl here. She came to the surface where the sun was glinting. She pulled herself onto a smooth rock. The trees towered all around her, and the tall cliffs of the valley towered above them, and enclosed them. Ann belonged here, in Yosemite.

Some boys were diving from the rocks a little ways down stream. Ann was wearing the two-piece swim suit she had gotten in Hawaii last summer. The boys were about her age, or a little older. She dove into the water again, and they could see her dive into the water, and that she was wearing a two-piece swim suit, and that she could dive as well as any boy.

But shadows fall early from the majestic cliffs of Yosemite. As soon as she was dry she strapped on her sandals and started up the bank. She opened the gate onto the hotel grounds. It was a secret gate, known only to a few. She started across the large expanse of lawn. The Awannee was a hotel of quiet grace and ageless wealth. This had been going on forever.

Barbara and their parents were sitting at a table on the great porch. It was time for her to dress for dinner. She took the room key and walked through the great sitting rooms. The rooms were furnished richly with chairs and couches upholstered in fabric designed by Indians, designed by Indians since the beginning of time. Great stone fireplaces rose to a ceiling that was tall and majestic, as Indians are.

In her room, Ann put on her plaid dress. It was simple, and it was sophisticated. It was a size five. All her other dresses were size seven, but this was size five. It showed she was thin.

When she came downstairs, Barbara and their parents were waiting for her at the door of the great dining hall. The maître d' showed them to their table. Everything was silver and fine linen and waiters in tuxedos. The food was, of course, exquisite. Ann hardly ate. But she enjoyed each course as it came. She enjoyed the luxury of not wanting to eat food that was totally attractive. She was lean but she was not hungry. In the back of her mind she knew that she had conquered appetite in order to allow leanness its whole flavor.

After dinner they walked out on the grass in their light wraps. A soprano voice was singing in the first dark before the rise of the moon. Then a voice, far away, but very clear, called out, "Let the fire fall!" And a great light appeared high up on Glacier Point. And in the dark they saw a waterfall of fire.

Ann and Barbara were released to go to the dance at Camp Curry. Barbara was worried that she wouldn't get asked to dance. Ann was asked to dance right away.

He was cool. They danced all night. His name was Bill. She hoped Barbara was dancing with somebody cool. If no one cool asked Barbara to dance and Barbara knew that somebody cool had danced with Ann how would she feel?

No one cool had asked Barbara to dance. Ann consoled her. The boys at the dance were a bunch of creeps. Except for Bill, but Bill was too young for Barbara. That's just an accident, Barbara, it doesn't mean that Ann is any cooler than you. It's just fate that she happens to be younger than you. Nothing was to spoil Ann's time now. Nothing could deny her leanness now that it had started.

Now in the morning when she toyed with her grapefruit she knew that she loved to eat, and this knowledge was like memory. For it was enough that the grapefruit was set in a dish which rested in ice held in a silver bowl. For she could feel her swim suit against her skin under her shirt. She was going to meet Bill in the pool in the stream after breakfast had run its full course. There was no necessity for her to hurry through her meal.

She let herself out of the secret gate, and as she made her way down the bank she saw Bill coming towards her from the opposite direction. He was coming from the campground. He and his parents were camping. They were all staying in a little trailer. Ann dove right into the water. She knew that anyone who stopped to consider might never go in. She did not go back to the Awannee for lunch.

Ann and Bill walked to the Indian caves. They crawled all the way inside the caves. Ann almost felt what it was like to be an Indian, and might have really felt it if there hadn't been other people—children and whole familes—climbing through and racing around the caves with them.

Then they heard the distant roar of a waterfall, and they let the sound draw them on through the trees until they were standing there, at the great rocks where the water was crashing. People who had come there on the trail were crowding the banks. Ann climbed out ahead of Bill over the rocks into the middle of the rushing stream.

That night in the great dining hall of the Awannee Ann knew that this would be the last night that she would be able not to eat. Tomorrow, they would be back in L.A. They hurried out into the night so as not to miss the firefall. Bill found Ann in the dark crowd. His arm stole around her, and as they lifted their faces up towards Glacier Point the fire flared, fell, and died.

Bill turned to Ann in the dark. "Where do you live?" he asked. "Beverly Hills," she said. "Beverly Hills? You really live in Beverly Hills? Do you live in a mansion?" "Oh, no, not really. Where do *you* live?" "I don't live too far from there. I live in Reseda," Bill said. "It's in the Valley." "Reseda?" Ann said. "Oh, really? I think I know where that is. I don't think it's too far." But Ann had glimpsed the tract homes of the Valley.

Back at home, everyone was getting ready for school. Then there was the Sunday School swim party—it was going to be at Eddie Hoffman's house. Billy Blackman was sure to be there. Ann hoped he would put popcorn down her swim suit again. Some friends of

Barbara's came over. They went out to the pool, but there was a little bit of chill in the air, so they decided not to go in. Ann washed her hair with Breck, and Barbara set it. They were sitting around in the kitchen devouring a diet cheesecake when the phone rang. It was a boy for Ann. Ann picked up the phone in her room and waited for Barbara to hang up the extension. It was Bill. Was Billy Blackman really calling her?

No, it was Bill from Yosemite. Bill from the Valley. He and his friends had driven over from Reseda and they were coming over.

Ann went out on the asphalt driveway to wait for them. Sometimes people missed their house. An old wreck of a car drove up. It didn't seem possible that this car had made it over Coldwater Canyon from the Valley. The doors fell open, and a bunch of boys with greasy hair and dirty tee shirts piled out of the car, shoving each other and laughing. One of them, theoretically, was Bill. She invited them in the house where they sat on the edge of the furniture.

It was very quiet in the house. The glare of the late afternoon sun slanted through the smog and through the clear windows. Barbara and her friends were hiding in her bedroom. The one who was Bill told Ann they were looking for movie stars' houses. Ann could hear giggles coming from Barbara's room. So she told the boys where they should go. Since she lived in Beverly Hills all the time she didn't want to go with them.

Palm Springs Again

ANN AND BARBARA begged their parents to take them to Palm Springs for Easter vacation, because that was the only way they could get there. They had to go, because everybody else was going. They had to stay at a certain hotel, because that was where everybody else was staying. Now they were on their way to Palm Springs, to the hotel where everybody would be. Ann had on a new pair of pants. They were pink and white check. She had bought them at jax where everybody bought their pants because they fit so tight and were so expensive. They arrived at the hotel, and started to see everyone prowling up and down the halls. As they checked into their rooms, Ann and Barbara pretended that they weren't with their parents. The beautiful blond girls were all there. Ann and Barbara were pretending they weren't with their parents, and Barbara was pretending she wasn't with Ann, because Ann was her younger sister. They did not swim, because they did not want to get their hair wet. Then they went into the coffee shop with their parents for lunch. They ordered diet specials, because they did not want to burst the zippers on their pants. Ann and Barbara could see the beautiful blond girls sitting across the room with the most handsome boys. They leaned back in the booth, hoping that nobody would see that they were there with their parents. Their parents did not seem to notice.

That night, they left the hotel to go to a movie with their parents. They hurried down the hall so that no one would see them leaving with their parents. All the beautiful blond girls were in the hallway. They were all wearing tight pants from jax. They were going into the rooms of the handsome popular boys. They were having parties in these rooms.

The movie they went to was *A Summer Place*, which starred Sandra Dee, who was a beautiful blond girl who wore pants from jax, didn't have to worry if her hair got wet, and never worried about bursting a zipper. Sandra Dee was in love with a handsome popular boy. He got her pregnant, and Sandra Dee had a lot of trouble. Ann wished that she was Sandra Dee. When the lights came on at the end of the movie she started to cry. She was not crying because the movie had a sad ending. She was crying because she was secretly Sandra Dee trapped in the reality of a movie theater with the lights on with her parents who thought that she was Ann.

No one saw her cry, and hopefully, no one saw her leave the movie theater with Barbara and her parents. She walked back to the hotel with her head bent against the desert wind and her hands holding her hair in place.

Transcontinental Cadillac

WITH DILIGENCE, honesty, and integrity, Ann's father had striven in the land of free enterprise to amass a fortune of considerable size. Where all men are created equal Ann's father had created a business which now, because of progress, had become a corporation. Out of nothing. Here in the most modern nation in the world his own daughters had never stood in a train station.

They flew. For it's hi hi hee in the land of lib-er-ty. Or they drove in the car. That was all they knew. They had never been further east than Arizona. He himself had never pushed back behind Nebraska, and now the two-week vacation he had promised himself was coming up. He had earned it striving unceasingly all year to provide a better life for his wife and kids. He was lucky to be living in America. So he would take two weeks off and take the whole family east to see the birthplace of the nation which allowed them to be born. They would see Central Park after dark and set foot on Plymouth Rock. They would see the U.S.A. The right way. They would pick up a Cadillac at the factory in Detroit where it's cheaper and drive it back across the fruited plain to L.A. That was the game plan.

From California to the New York Harbor on American Airlines.

"Oh, say, can you see?" the pilot said. "That's the Grand Canyon sliding way beneath you." Ann looked down. Now she was looking up. She was in a stone canyon. She was being pushed off the curb. She was going to be hit by a car. Now she was looking down from the top of the Empire State Building.

Then, after being moved around underground, they popped out on Wall Street. Here in Trinity Churchyard they discovered the headstone of Alexander Hamilton. It was *the* Alexander Hamilton. What was he doing here?

The show was just letting out, and they were giving their regards to Broadway. Who would have suspected that they would have to see such great shows in such beat-up theaters? They were standing on a street corner looking for a taxi with the wind blowing dirt in their faces. New York was a nice place to visit, but where had everybody gone who lived here? The town was empty. It was the Fourth of July.

They left from Grand Central Station on the Congressional to Washington. Ann had learned how the great railroads—the Short Line, the B. and O., the Pennsylvania, and the Reading—had made it possible for the entire continent to be claimed and tamed. And how, even though they had done this, nobody cared for the railroads anymore, and they were cast off. This was Ann's first ride on a railroad. It was the train all the congressmen rode. It was filthy.

Washington itself was filthy beyond their wildest dreams. And in the filth they saw all the shrines and monuments of liberty and freedom. There was more here on their plate than they could possibly eat during their short stay at the Mayflower Hotel, so they saw what they could of the Smithsonian full of aircraft and bombers, and the tomb of the unknown soldier who stands for every American. They saw the site of Kennedy's inauguration and Dali's painting of the Last Supper in the National Gallery.

They saw where great Americans had lived—Mt. Vernon, the Lee-Curtis house. In order to get in they had to pay a small price.

To avoid having to pay for breakfast at the Mayflower they caught a breakfast flight to Boston. That is, they were supposed to get breakfast on the flight. The airline tried to discriminate against them by not having enough breakfasts for all of them. Ann's father told them that this was no way to run a business. He was going to demand his rights. Not because a breakfast in itself is significant, but because if rights aren't exercised they atrophy. He still didn't get any breakfast.

He got a refund at the airport in Boston. They had lost a bit of time, so they raced through Lexington and Concord in a rented car until finally they came to Plymouth Rock. A busload of Girl Scouts from South Pasadena had gotten there first, so they had to wait for the next tour. Finally, guides wearing pilgrim suits took their money and told them that the real Plymouth Rock was a little further up the coast.

They drove to Cape Cod where everyone was digging for clams and to Cape Ann to see the "first motif" they had so often seen painted. It was an excellent likeness. Ann liked it, but they couldn't stay, they had to get back to Boston to catch their flight out, but when they got there they couldn't leave anyway because their flight had been delayed. So, since they had a little time to kill, they drove across the Charles river looking for Harvard, and drove around and around looking for a place to park, and made it back to the plane just in time and flew to Detroit where they went right to the Caddy factory and drove west.

Now, in their own brand new air-conditioned Cadillac with all the electric windows raised they were driving down the Indiana Turnpike. They stopped to pay, and drove on and passed through Chi-ca-go and stopped at Skokie, Illinois. They spent the next day in a motel room in Skokie, Illinois, because there was nothing to see in Skokie, Illinois. But they had to spend the day there because Ann's father had business there.

They crossed the great Mississipi River at Dubuque, Iowa, stopping only long enough to see the home of U. S. Grant, which was well worth their while, as they didn't have to pay to see it. And to think that they had had to pay to see Lee's house.

They drove through the Dakotas, through the badlands, and they went to Mt. Rushmore where the colossal faces of the American giants looked down upon them. And over the miserable roads of Wyoming they forged on on their padded upholstery and as night fell they pulled into Cody, Wyoming, home of Buffalo Bill Cody, who had been famous for fighting the Indians. The Indians used every part of the buffalo. Buffalo Bill had gone into show business. He used Indians in every part of his act.

The next day they drove into Yellowstone, but they drove

through it quickly as they had heard how commercial it was. All of America was here feeding the bears and courting destruction. They were hurrying on to a place undefiled and undiscovered.

By midmorning they had reached eternity. Oh sublime majesty! The Grand Tetons rising above Jackson Lake. Here in a new land they would rest safe at last from the toils and turmoil of the old world. By day they walked the nature trails looking for moose, and as they hiked around the shores of Jenny Lake, it was as if no one had ever walked these trails before, it was as if they were walking on sacred ground.

They couldn't stay here forever, they had to push on across the great American desert to Las Vegas. And out of the sterility of the desert it rose before them like a mirage. A place absolutely without history.

They caught some first-rate acts in a very glamourous and expensive night club. Then, as Mother and Father were going to stay up and gamble, Ann and Barbara went up to their rooms. These were not the rooms they were supposed to have. The hotel had mislaid their reservation, and now they were full up. But Ann's father had sent in a deposit, and he had brought his cancelled check with him. So the hotel had finally come up with this—the honeymoon suite. Barbara went in and switched on the t.v., and Ann took a dip in the pink heart-shaped swimming pool which took up most of the living space.

P. S.

ANN WANTED TO GO to Palm Springs without her parents, but they wouldn't let her. By the time she would get there she would be a beautiful blond girl. Well, she wouldn't really be a beautiful blond girl, but no one would be able to tell, and wonderful things would happen to her. She would be able to act naturally in the part, because she had studied the role. All day long she would be admired lying by the pool, and at night she would go to a party in one of the handsome popular boys' rooms, and at the party one of the most handsome popular boys—she didn't go as far as thinking that it would be *the* most handsome popular boy—but a handsome enough boy would come up to her in the dark and kneel by her chair and say "I love you. I have loved you secretly for three months." Then the lights would come on and everyone would know. They would beam approval and they would take it for granted. There would always be a few people, of course, who were secretly jealous.

But Ann knew her parents didn't want her to go because they pictured her chasing fat ugly middle-aged men down the hallways and sitting in motel rooms with her head tilted back and the whiskey pouring down her throat. She knew her parents saw her standing with the lights out naked in a really cheap motel room with a neon light going on and off outside coming in at every pulse through the dirty venetian blinds with a naked man who was also standing.

So Ann appealed to her parents' reason. They were not the sort of people who wanted to have an unpopular daughter.

They let her go with Doreen. Doreen was not actually her friend. She was the daughter of a friend of her mother's—the one she played mahjong with. Doreen was dumb, but she was useful. She had a Corvair.

Doreen drove the Corvair at ninety miles an hour on the way to Palm Springs, but that would not get them to Palm Springs any sooner than they got there. They checked into the same hotel where everybody had stayed last year, just like last year. During the year the hotel had gotten a bit shabby. For one thing, it was familiar. It was not better. They went down to the coffee shop for lunch. Ann looked for someone she knew who was there with their parents. She did not see anyone. She did not see anyone she knew period. Everyone—or the few who were in Palm Springs—was at a new hotel on the other side of town. Perhaps she and Doreen would go over there later and sit in the lobby.

They left Palm Springs for the last time on Sunday and arrived in L.A. a few hours later.

The Three and a Half Grand Tour

A YOUNG LADY is not properly finished in America until she's been abroad. So now that Mr. and Mrs. Godwin's daughter Ellenor had turned sixteen it was time to take her to Europe. They would take her with them this summer, never considering the expense. That was a given. What was money to them? They had money bags of rare coins in trust for their daughter in their closet. Mr. Godwin had once opened the closet to show them to his dear daughter's best friend—a fine girl, really a good influence on his daughter, almost a part of the family. Then they walked down the hall, past the etchings by Matisse and Chagall on the wall, past Edna, the live-in maid, bringing the poodles back from their shampoo, out to the living room where Mrs. Godwin, exquisitely dressed, was playing a little Chopin at the grand piano.

Mr. and Mrs. Godwin's daughter, naturally, was appreciative of the proposal. She was, already at her age, familiar with art and culture. She was dying for romance and adventure. If she didn't jump up and down for glee it was only because she didn't want to startle her parents who were easily startled and because she wondered how much romance and adventure she would have traveling alone with her parents. If only her best friend could come with them!

To take this girl along would be a large responsibility for Mr. and Mrs. Godwin. But their daughter could share a hotel room with this girl, and they wouldn't have to have a cot brought into their own room. Their daughter would profit from having a companion on the journey.

They didn't imagine, however, that the girl's parents, who had never been to Europe themselves and never went to the opera, would consent to give her this rich experience. It would only cost these people $3,500 to send her along with them. Didn't they have any shame?

When Ann asked her parents if she could go with the Godwins they let her know what a big sacrifice this would be for them. They didn't want any less for Ann than Ellen Godwin's parents wanted for *her*. The expense was nothing to sneeze at. They would let her go—on two conditions: that she would not imbibe any alcoholic beverages of any description, and that she would not spend a penny over her hundred dollar allowance for purchases. So Ann's father arranged a business meeting with the Godwins, and while Mr. Godwin was signing the papers, Ann and Ellen crept down the hall to Ellen's room where they jumped up and down for glee.

So this was Europe. It was very thrilling. To think they were so far away. It was purely elegant. One hotel surpassed another. Silver, mirrors, fine upholstery. Elevator boys.

A most gracious people. They knew how to serve. In perfect taste.

They ate the most elegant food of each elegant country. In Spain they dined at ten o'clock and had footstools. Some of the food was so elegant it made them sick. Cloudberries in Norway. Lox for eight dollars a pound. Ann was following the Godwins down the stairs into one of the world's most elegant French restaurants, *Malmaison*, in Glasgow. She sensed someone coming towards her, looked up, and was dazzled when she saw *herself* in her perfect paisley Ban-lon dress. It was only a mirror, but too late. Ann was falling downstairs into *Malmaison*.

With perfect manners she was lifted and dusted and led to the table where the Godwins sat beaming as discreet violins started up on the interior balcony.

This is what she had had to order the night before. *Haggis.* They had gone to so much trouble to prepare it. What was it, exactly? She took the news bravely. Was this not what it was to have adventure? Blood in guts.

In France they ordered their steak *sans beurre* and in Italy, *senza burro.* The Godwins knew their way around. If you let them, these Europeans would put butter on everything.

So this was what it was like to be in a completely different place, Ann thought, eating *spaghetti* in London. This was the Old World. Queens had slept in these old beds.

Layers of time. Ann is riding with the Godwins in a bus to see an old church in old Norway. Everyone on the bus is Cockney and singing songs. One Cockney shows Ellen's father what he has in his pocket. It is a ball-point pen. Suspended in the top of the pen is a small woman in evening dress. "Very nice," Mr. Godwin says. Then the Cockney inverts the pen, and laughing, the woman sheds her gown. He puts it back in his pocket. He has dozens of these things with him, he tells Mr. Godwin. "Never come over 'ere wivout 'em."

When in Rome they shipped their coats back home. They were sitting eating lunch on the verandah of the hotel restaurant overlooking the Spanish Steps. A handsome waiter was running a knife all over the fuzzy peach on Ann's plate. Just then the most handsome man in the world strode into the dining room. It was the elevator boy. He was the occasion of Ann and Ellen's frequent goings up and down. Now he was coming over to their table. He was coming over to them. He wished to tell the *signorinas* that he had just been in their room. He had been there to deliver the little packages of shoes they had been expecting. Ann and Ellen looked at each other. Each was seeing with horror and delight what *he* must have seen when he entered their room—their *bras* draped across the back of the chair! Just then the waiter pulled the skin from Ann's peach in one piece.

For Ann and Ellen, to be in Europe was to no longer be in themselves. *Mesdemoiselles!* the sailors called after them. The girls didn't respond. *Miss?* the sailors suggested. Ann and Ellen walked on. *Señoritas?* they persisted. *Señorinas?* Wrong again.

Frökena? they offered. Close, but no cigar. *Chinoises???* Ann and Ellen had reached the edge of the canal. The man in the gondola tipped his straw hat. *GONdola? GonDOLa?*

They were seeing here in person what they had only enjoyed before in books. *The Night Watch* in Holland. *Winged Victory* at the *Louvre.* The gray sky moving elongated over Toledo in the *Prado.* The endless mess too high up on the ceiling of the *Sistine Chapel.*

They were really seeing each country because they were seeing the people of each country. They were staying with a real family in Manchester. Mr. and Mrs. Usher, friends of the Godwins. Ann and Ellen stood on the lawn in the drizzle watching little Usher in short pants bounce around in a three-legged race. Then the Ushers drove them around through places truly wonderful, and then just into Wales. "There's a typical *Welshman* for you," Mr. Usher said. Ann looked at the man standing by the hedge examining its leaves. He had his back to them. His legs were slightly spread, his head was bowed, and his hands were in front of him. "Do you think he thinks he's really fooling us?" Mr. Usher asked, driving on.

They had gotten into the habit of drinking beer before going to sleep each night. In the dream, Ann is in a strange country looking for the bathroom because she has to pee. When she gets in she sees both men and women squatting over pots. Ann doesn't think she can do it here, in front of all of them. But if it is the local custom . . . ?

Ann writes home to her real family and tells them all about her trip. She wants them to know what a wonderful time she is having . . .

> ski sweater . . . Norway . . . $20.00
> watch with spare watch bands . . . Switzerland . . . $30.50
> 3 charms evocative of 3 countries . . . $34.00
> purse (beaded) . . . Paris . . . $15.00
> purse (fur) . . . $4.00
>
>   With the purchase of some film I have concluded my $100 allowance. I think I have bought wisely thus far, but there are still certain things which I might want to purchase, such as a bracelet for my charms, some

other charms, Italian shoes, gloves, or maybe jewelry, and maybe something of value completely unanticipated. Will you please write and tell if I can buy anything else? I don't wish to go against your wishes. I love you and know that you know best. Did Grandma get the handkerchiefs? Please give my love to everyone . . .

To be in Europe was to be totally without cares. All Ann and Ellen had to do was wash out their underwear every night and sit back and listen to the music. A Viennese movie of *Der Rosenkavalier* in London. *La Bohème* in the Paris Opera House. Something minor yet remembered anyway in the *Baths of Caracalla*. From where they sat sipping *Cinzano* in the *piazza* they could hear several bands going at once.

"Take us to the *Ritz Hotel*," Mr. Goodwin commanded the Castillian cab driver. He was inscrutable and self-contained. He drove them to the *Rex Theater*. Apparently, that was what they had asked for.

The excursion cruiser sailed on the fiord. The *Bateau Mouche* sailed on the Seine. Nobody knew how to drive. If they sat here long enough, everybody in the world would pass by.

Ellen's cousin Harry from *New Jersey* passed by just then, spotted them, and came back and sat down at their table. He was actually living here in Paris, in a little garret room two floors up from the bathroom. He would be their guide and show them everything they wanted to see, such as *Montmartre* where foreigners in berets were painting *Sacŕ Coeur*. "Don't buy," Harry said. When Mr. and Mrs. Godwin were safely tucked into bed at the *Prince de Galles,* Harry took Ann and Ellen out to see the real Paris. He took them to a cellar on the Left Bank. When their eyes adjusted to the light of the real Paris, they saw that they were in a kind of nightclub. A single Negro man was singing *le jazz* on the stage. As the number finished, Harry put up his palm to stop Ann and Ellen from clapping. "*Non, comme ci,*" he said, starting to snap his fingers. Indeed, everyone in the club was avidly snapping their fingers to show their appreciation. Ann and Ellen started to snap. They didn't think Harry would really return home to engineering school next week.

Water flowed under the bridge. Snow melted in the alps. The

sun blazed on the Mediterranean. Ann and Ellen dug their toes into the sand and flung their heads back. They were provocative in their bikinis. The beach was packed. Everyone was wearing bikinis. A strange man was standing over them.

"Excuse, please, you girls from the U.S.?"

"Us?"

"Yes, please, do you know Mrs. Florence Hilopsi?"

"Who?"

"Mrs. Florence Hilopsi, my cousin, in Toledo, Ohio."

"How are you spelling that?"

"Please, to Mrs. Florence Hilopsi, actually the cousin of my wife, best regards from Mario."

Ann and Ellen got up and walked into the sea. Two swarthy men with flashing black eyes swam up to them, and followed them back to the shore where they offered to take their picture. One of the men posed with an arm around each girl's naked waist. Ann and Ellen each put an arm around his dark smooth back, and held each other, while the other man took a long time with the focus. Then he changed places with his partner.

The men wanted to know if the girls wanted to go to the cabaret with them that night.

"Yes." Mr. and Mrs. Godwin would never let them.

That night, Ann and Ellen went to bed, got up and got dressed. Then they pressed their ears to the door which led into Mr. and Mrs. Godwin's room. First there was nothing, then there was snoring. Ann and Ellen tip-toed out of the room and down the hall.

They didn't go to the cabaret after all. After all, Mr. and Mrs. Godwin wouldn't have wanted them to. The men wanted to show them the beach by night.

It was nothing like the beach by day. It was deserted. The man who had chosen Ann took her hand. Ellen and her man were walking ahead of them on the beach.

Now they had disappeared. So Ann let the man who had chosen her out of everyone else in the world put his hand under her dress.

"Tell me about yourself," he said, pulling back the elastic of her suspants as they walked along.

"Well, you should know I'm a virgin," Ann said, looking straight ahead. "I'm not going all the way."

"And yet you let me . . . ?" he asked, in a strange accent. Ann realized that she was not obeying the local custom. She did not have to. She was free. The country she came from was strange and mysterious.

Just then they were knocked apart. They had walked into the under-structure of the life-guard tower. Ann smoothed down her skirt. This was whispering she was hearing. She thought she saw two forms embracing on the top of the tower.

"Ellen?" she called. With the sound of her voice the forms pushed apart.

"*Ciao*, Ann," Ellen called. "We're up here. We're guarding lives."

They were afraid it was time to go back.

Now Ellen was about to turn out the light. Their bras and stockings still attached to garters were draped over the satin striped furniture. Their eyemakeup was smeared on the rococo dressing table.

"What did you think of those creeps?" Ellen asked, tieing her hairnet.

"I could've done without them," Ann said.

"Mine tried to French-kiss me," Ellen said.

"No!" Ann said to Ellen's reflection in the silver-gilt mirror.

"Ee-yu!" Ellen said. "Yik. You got the cuter one."

"Not cute enough," Ann said, getting under the covers.

"I'm dead," Ellen said.

"We're really going to be dead tomorrow," Ann said, and she turned out the light.

Ann found Beverly Hills a very strange place. It hadn't changed a bit. It was hard to get used to. Ann's parents wondered in front of her if they had spoiled her. She explained to them that it was nothing personal; she was suffering from culture shock. She lay around listlessly in her room listening to Edith Piaf sing "*Non, je ne regrette rien.*" This was the beginning of her senior year, the year she should be nostalgic about for the rest of her life.

South of the Border Between High School and College

MOTHER AND FATHER were waving. Danny was waving and leaning out the glass door blowing kisses. Ann saw them through the double glass of the window. She waved back, but she didn't suppose any of them could really see her because it was darker inside the plane than it was out.

Maybe they did see her. She was crying. Not that it mattered. She wasn't really crying, she just had tears in her eyes. If they saw her they would think that she was sad to be leaving Danny for two months. Let them. She wasn't. She despised Danny. He was her steady date, but it was clear to her how little they cared for each other every time Danny felt compelled to tell her he loved her. One could suppose this was because his mother had been married five times or because they lived in a very demanding community.

In the five months that Ann had been dating Danny she had learned all the sports car terms. He always asked her how many feet of rubber she wanted him to lay when he "patched out" in his Vette. He was obviously operating on the principle that Ann should be impressed by the fact that he drove a Corvette. But actually Ann despised Corvettes. The last boy she had dated before Danny had driven a Corvette. Admittedly, that was why she had dated him—she was gold digging. Not that she thought well of herself for doing it, but she hadn't really had any choice. No one else was asking her out.

Vette #1 had given her presents. There were two stuffed pink dogs. They would always remind her of him. There had been a bottle of expensive perfume. It smelled cheap on her. He had said to her, "I bet that you weigh more than I do." She had hated him. Since she weighed more than he did she should feel grateful that he wanted to date her. She shouldn't object to the fact that he was a scrawny, skinny little twerp if he drove a car that was small and powerful enough. Enough to let him park the Corvette up on Mulholland Drive and grope at her over the gear shift. She despised Corvettes and what their owners thought they could do to her.

She had despised herself while he was trapping her alone in the living room of his father's mansion. She had been wearing Barbara's red wool skirt because it was a size eight, because she had wanted to prove to him that she didn't weigh more than he did, and the lining was about to rip. He had one hand under her skirt and was pulling brutally on one of her nipples with the other. She must get a hold of herself, she must stop this somehow. She mustn't let him know that he had actually been able to hurt her. Was this all that she could expect from life? He told her that his uncle had produced one of the biggest grossing movies of all time. Was she supposed to jump for joy at this? What did it mean, actually? That he would be able to get her in at half price at a matinee if the movie ever came around again? This was actually worse than not having a date.

And so finally she had snipped Vette #1 out of her life and had thrown him in the waste-paper basket. Then she had sat home on Saturday night not answering the phone so that no one would know she wasn't on a date. She was getting desperate. This was her senior year. She was going to need someone to take her to the Big Game, the Senior Breakfast, and the Senior Prom. Her mother had told her about girls who weren't invited to these things. It was around then that she had started talking to Danny in her communications class. Soon enough, they were passing notes.

Ann's problem was that she had never needed a boyfriend who went to her own school before. Her first love had come from another school. In fact, she had met him in Sunday School. Then one afternoon at the Sunday School swim party he had put popcorn down her swim suit. She couldn't believe it was happening to her at last. And then her dream came true—Billy Blackman took her in his arms and kissed her. And then a strange thing happened—his tongue came into her mouth. He was French-kissing her! So that's what it was! What would people think? Billy Blackman had chosen her to French-kiss. She hoped she was good at it.

The next weekend they had gone out on a date. And from the back seat where she sat with Billy she watched Billy's father watching them in the rear-view mirror as he drove them to the movies.

Perhaps Ann's eyes were moist now behind the double glass because of the movies. In the movies, eyes are always moist behind the glass, and so Ann's tears were in no way suspect.

One afternoon she had gone over to Billy Blackman's house to dance and listen to records. She was wearing a new pair of hip-hugger pants from jax which fit very tight. Her father hadn't censored them when he drove her over, because she was also wearing a large white overblouse. But her overblouse rode up as she danced, and Billy saw them then. Later, when they were in the hallway, she reached over and put her hand on the lump in his pants. He left it there in awe. Then he asked her how she had known to do that. "Oh, I just knew," she said, wondering what it was she was doing.

On the night of her sixteenth birthday, Billy Blackman drove himself over to her house while her parents were out at a card party and her sister was out on a blind date. He was supposed to drive her up to where her parents were. But it was, after all, her sixteenth birthday. One had a sixteenth birthday only once in a lifetime. So she found a bottle of champagne in the pantry. And after they had drunk it the idea came to them to take a moonlight swim.

No moon shone through the night smog, but an underwater light lit up their limbs. Billy's tongue came into Ann's mouth, and as his finger moved inside of her she reached out and put her hand around him as he bobbed back and forth before her in the water. Her legs twined around his, and he moved slowly against her lips. Was she in danger of losing her virginity? Surely it wasn't possible while swimming.

They got out of the pool and raced through the cool night to the house, where together they took a warm bath. Then they dried themselves with one towel, as if only Ann had had a bath, but Billy followed Ann into her bedroom, where she had to get dressed quickly, as her parents were expecting her. So they lay down on Ann's bed kissing and touching, and the penis was still there. This had to stop somewhere because if it didn't, Ann would lose her virginity. And she couldn't very well lose her virginity on her childhood bed. The single bed her parents had provided for her all these years. The bed she had lain in night after night in her shorty pajamas whispering that she was in her shorty pajamas to Billy Blackman who breathed heavily back into the phone while her parents slept in the other part of the house. Her parents! Her parents would wonder where she was.

They got dressed quickly, and took a tube of toothpaste with them to disguise the champagne on their breath, and when Ann walked up to the card table where her parents were sitting she was able to hold it nonchalantly in one hand.

The next day her father found the empty champagne bottle in the trash and forbade her to ever see Billy Blackman again. How could she! Hadn't they sent her abroad last summer? Did she think they would let her apply to Berkeley after this? The extension was taken out of her room. She was grounded.

She sat on her bed and outlined the situation in her notebook:

Crime and Punishment
(Lessons to Be Learned Therefrom)

A.
1. An unknown crime cannot be punished.
2. Punishment is no fun.
3. Not to tell is lying.
4. Lying is profitable.
5. *One should lie.*

B.
1. Crimes are bad (completely).
2. There is only one side to each coin.
3. There is no gray between white and black.

C.
1. Syllogism: Sending you abroad was a great sacrifice.

A person who is so fortunate is less excusable to crime than a poor kid.
Conclusion: All rich kids are white (good).
Quandary: We are only middle class. Can't I be tainted?

D.
1. Punishment makes one good by instilling
   a. fear
   b. bitterness
2. And this punishment will be specifically à propos to the crime as the accused
   a. will be dateless
   b. will be friendless
   c. will be bored
   d. will be lonely
   e. will have no chance for fun or relaxation
   f. will love the judges more
   g. will be able to contribute more to the family life
      1.) by being melancholy
      2.) by throwing crying spells
      3.) by being sullen
      4.) by being more secretive
      5.) by having to be driven and picked up
   Conclusion:
      I agree punishment is in order—but like Lao Tse—in moderation.
      As for Berkeley, nothing can stop me from leaving home next year. If you continue to keep me bodily home my soul and my spirit—my animation and ambition—will idle away, just leaving my shell, my hollow empty shell—I'll be a hollow man. (T. S. Eliot)

It was shortly after her parents found the notebook that they let her accept a date with Eddie Hoffman. After all, they knew Eddie Hoffman's parents. Eddie Hoffman was in Ann's Sunday School class. They knew Ann didn't really like Eddie Hoffman.

Eddie Hoffman told her parents politely what movie they were going to, and what time they would be home. Eddie and Ann walked out to the car. Eddie opened the door for her and she got in.

The couple they were doubling with were sitting in the back seat. When they got around the corner Eddie stopped the car. Then Ann changed seats with the girl who was in the back seat. And she got in the back seat with Billy Blackman.

Instead of driving them to the movies, Eddie drove to his uncle's house in Topanga Canyon. His uncle was away on vacation, so they had the house to themselves. Eddie and his date built a fire in the living room, while Billy showed Ann the master bedroom. Ann put her hand on Billy's zipper. "We mustn't," she said. "Don't worry," Billy breathed in her ear. His hand was under her blouse unfastening her bra. "No," she said, taking his penis in her mouth. "I promise," he said from beneath her, and he parted the lips of her vagina with his tongue. "Oh, God," she said. Surely she couldn't lose her virginity like this. Then his face swam towards her, and she was pulling him to her saying "Stop! We have to stop! Please!"

For a moment Billy lay still. Then he kissed Ann on the forehead and stood up. And with his back to her he pulled on his pants. "The movie's over now!" Eddie called up the stairs.

Then Eddie drove them home. Billy walked her to the door. They could go no further.

Ann had never been south of the border before. Perhaps her eyes were moist now behind the double glass out of a fear of the unknown.

Howsoever, Ann's eyes weren't moist for very long. She had started to draw in her sketch pad the grotesque figures which she always drew. Some people, when they looked in Ann's sketch pad, said that she was warped. She always felt complimented.

Wasn't it warped of her to choose to leave Danny for two months? Yes, her parents might think so. But, on the other hand, she had a terrible wanderlust. She needed to broaden her perspectives. She told people that she wanted to go places so that they wouldn't suspect she wanted to go away.

She was always in terror that her mother was finding things out about her. For example, she would be lying in bed reading *La Nausée* in the quiet of the space of the night when she would hear the front door far away open and close. Then she would hear the door slide open to Barbara's room. Soon there were other footsteps coming through the house. Now Mother was in Barbara's room, in Barbara's room right behind the thin wall against which Ann was lying in her narrow bed. And she would hear them talking while Barbara undressed, and she would hear Barbara telling Mother *everything* about the date she had just been on. Ann didn't want to listen. She didn't want to tell Mother all about the date *she* had just been on with Danny. She would rather read *La Nausée* than even think about it. What did it matter? She had bought her hat for the Senior Breakfast.

She needed to get away. Father was always stopping her at the door as she was going out on a date and making her go back to change into a longer dress. Promising in front of her date to break both her arms if she came home a minute past her curfew. Letting her know how much he liked Danny, how glad he was that she had a decent boyfriend at last. Ann had this to go away from. Perhaps she was looking for something. Maybe she was looking for herself. She liked to call it adventure.

There was a fly in the window next to her. It buzzed around doing whatever flies do in their odious ways. Ann wondered if it knew it was about to travel fifteen hundred miles. It would never see any of its fellow flies again. Not that it would notice. Ann didn't really suppose that flies had friends. She couldn't stand them herself. Ann glanced at Barbara sitting next to her. Barbara was looking a little airsick.

Ann opened her sketch pad again. Start with an eye. Take the eyebrow into the nose. A chinless, pockmarked, hideous human specimen. She saw them all the time, through the faces which she looked through, why not draw them? Below Ann's nose Baja California was going by. Great brown bogs appeared.

It was only by accident that she was here at all. She was only here, actually, because of Barbara. Barbara was going to Mexico to study Spanish, and Ann was going as her duenna. Barbara had chosen Spanish as her language in high school, and Ann had chosen French. What if everyone spoke Spanish and Ann could only speak French? What if Ann couldn't communicate with anyone? Suddenly there was a jungle.

The runway came up to meet them. They had stopped. Ann's hair curled up. They were in Guadalajara.

They were being driven from the airport by Manuel, the chauffeur. The street was black with neon lights. They came to a broad avenue. Manuel opened the gate.

Maria, the oldest daughter of the family, spoke the welcome of her parents in English, welcomed them to the house. Her house was their house. She was glad they had come. Two years ago, another student had come to study at the summer University. This student had also stayed in their house. This student had come from Pasadena. Because of this student, Maria felt a great feeling for Californians. This student had been a boy. This student had kissed her. She had never been kissed before or since by any boy. She will always wait for Glenn—this boy from a fine family in Pasadena— to return. There is a possibility that she is engaged. Last summer, Glenn's mother honored her family with a visit. She had stayed much longer than they had hoped. Perhaps—no, she was sure that Glenn himself would return some summer soon. Maria was twenty-five. She had spoken to other boys who had come to call on her through the gate only, and never after ten o'clock. She welcomed them to Guadalajara, the provincial capital, second only to Pasadena.

Ann and Barbara were shown to their rooms, and the next day they started school. Then one day Ann couldn't remember what day it was and she realized it was *Martes*. Now that she was in Mexico there were no more Tuesdays. She was in the bathroom trying to wash the green paint out from under her fingernails. That made her think of Ellen, who always said green was the most important color in the world. Ann always said green was the most important color, too, because they were best friends. She went down to the courtyard, and balancing her stationery box on her lap she wrote in green ink:

Martes

Dear Ellen,

Only this morning my hands were a verdant shade up to my forearms! That is because this week our landscape class goes to the Barrancas. We go in a bus that bears the name of our school, "Cervantes," in black letters on its flank. I love to watch the crumbling adobe walls, the mujeres wearing shawls, and the dirty staring children go by out the window. The Barrancas! You walk out with your easel to a point and look into a giant canyon of green. How can I begin to paint it?

I painted the children in the churchyard of Zapopan! As you know, I have never had a real love for children—but these niños—carrying my palette—sticking lighted matches into ant-hills—so beautiful—so dirty—so eager to be painted!

How can I tell you? Guadalajara is the image of inspiration for me. Oh, the wrought iron bars on the windows!

Even school is great. After class, we all sit in the courtyard and socialize. I soch it up with Scott, (surfer, Cal frosh), Henry, (U. of Arizona—gorgeous), Brad Block, (frosh, U. of Arizona), and his brother Bart, (a Beta at the University of Arizona. We're best of friends!) And then there's John (Stanford) and Jan, (a boy). Not to mention Rodolfo, who invited us to his private museum. He says he wants to date the "gringas libras." Rodolfo is a good friend of Raùl's.

I'm sitting now in the house of my Mexican family. It is muy rico. Our father is a general in the Mexican air force, so there are huge propellers over the staircase. Right now, El General is in Mexico City—with his mistress! When he's gone, the Señora spends all day with the cook. All the husbands have mistresses here, and all the wives are fat.

But when El General is here he calls us downstairs to breakfast singing, "She'll be combing round the mountain when she combs." He's teaching us to speak in Español. ("To eat" is "comer.") Spanish is really a musical language.

Everyone is very friendly and helpful. We date almost every night. Barbara is going steady with a really bitchin' guy named Juan. She thinks she's going to marry him. Can you imagine? We go to night clubs and drink Black Russians and dance to "Ojos Verdes." I've been to five different night clubs already and once to the auto cine. I've also seen a cock fight, and I've been to the procession of the Virgin. That was on my first date with Raùl.

I've never seen such a gorgeous selection of boys, but

I'm in love with Raùl. I'm so *attracted* to him. When I see him I get all nervous and just melt. He's almost twenty, but he calls me a chica. Oh Raùl! When I hear his name I get all excited and twitchy.

Danny's only written me two letters since I've been here. The rat fink!

Now I've got to get this paint off my fingers. Raùl will be here any minute!

      Love,

      Your Mexican sister,

        Ann

Ann sealed the letter and washed her hands. Then she put on her low-cut summer date dress and her high heels and walked down the spiral staircase, past the small parlor where the Señora sat doing découpage on cigarette boxes with the cook, and out to the front room where Raùl stood up smiling as she entered. He helped her into his car, and they drove through the moonlight to the little fishing village of Ajijic. There the rain beat down on the cobblestones while they sang and danced in the cabaret. One day, Ann would return here as an artist. But tonight she would dance in the rain. That night, Raùl had a surprise for Ann. It was no silly stuffed dog. It was a bottle of gin.

The next day Raùl came for Ann in the daytime. She told Barbara they were going to a soccer game and then for a refresco. It was not the truth. The truth found them driving to Raùl's family home in the Country Club Estates.

There Raùl showed Ann the pool in the center of his garden. It was round like a well and deep, made of stones, with flowers growing at the edge, as if naturally. Ann wanted to go in. Raùl was taking off his shirt.

"But I didn't bring my swim suit," she said.

"It is no matter," Raùl said. There is no one here." Now the rest of his clothes fell to the grass, and he stood for a moment in plain sight. Then he dove in.

He called to her from the center of the pool. "Do not hesitate. The water is warm."

Ann slipped off one sandal and dipped her foot in the pool. The water was a delicious concoction. She was sliding through it toward him. His strong legs were twining around hers under water. She was in danger of going under.

So Raùl helped her out. He led her across the vivid green lawn to the house. There was nobody home. He was leading her down a bright corridor. Sunlight was beaming down through clear windows. He was kissing her. Her arms were around him. He was leading her into a bedroom where he pulled back the covers from the bed. Now lying on the cool sheet his mouth was moving all over her, and twining her legs around him Ann called out in words she could not be responsible for knowing.

How could she be responsible for what she was doing? This wasn't even her country. In one sense, she *was* going for a refresco. No one would suspect that she was actually screwing. To the world she was just leaving the soccer game, and the refresco had not yet begun. She wouldn't want people to jump to the conclusion that she was losing her virginity in Mexico. If they ever accused her of it she would deny it righteously. She knew that what she was doing was not wrong. The truth was on her side.

The truth was that she had already lost it. She had lost it to the Big Game, the Senior Prom, and the Senior Breakfast, where her hat had looked ridiculous on her head.

She had not even enjoyed these events. But she had gotten through them. She had used Danny to get her through. What annoyed her was the thought that he probably thought he had been using her. Because, as if in payment, but in the name of love, he had exacted her virginity. He had pressed her and pressed her, until she couldn't think of any other way to say no.

She had said no again and again to Billy Blackman. Now what did it get her? Danny's prick in her mouth. She had taken it first out of a sense of social obligation. She had tried to protest that she didn't want it. But he didn't believe her. And why should he? She did want it. She was tormented with it.

And once it had started, there was no way of stopping. Danny started to leave his Corvette at home and started picking her up in his uncle's Woody. Ann's parents wished that Ann were more enthusiastic about Danny. Ann's mother warned her that she would lose him if she didn't watch out. He was the nicest boy she had ever dated. She had better be smart. Ann continued to despise herself.

Ideally, you are supposed to love the boy you give your flower to. So Ann couldn't tell anyone, not even Ellen, what she had done. In that way it had never happened. Not until now.

The next night Ann went with Raùl to a motel, all tiled in pink and green. In America, these colors would have seemed gross to Ann. But she was not in America. Raùl handed some paper money through a little wicket. Was this what it was to be cheap? She followed Raùl up the dark narrow stairs. No one could see you on the stairway. They went into a room filled by a bed.

The next day at dinner Ann sat toying with her food. Her family asked her if she was sick. She wondered if she was pregnant. "I don't know," she said. "Here, you better have some tequila," they said. Arriba, abajo, al fresco, intesco, and she downed it. Then she excused herself from the table and crawled up the spiral staircase under the propellers which were going round and round to the landing. As she started crawling across the tiles to the bathroom she noticed Manuel, the houseboy, leaning on his mop. He was laughing mutely. She looked down and saw the spots of blood she was trailing across the tiles. Ann felt better already. What she had done had not been wrong. Here was her period like a reward.

She felt well enough, in fact, to go out with Raùl to the auto cine the next night. Instead, Raùl took her to a little house, which was an actual love nest. It belonged to Raùl's brother, who wasn't nesting there that night. Raùl picked up a record and put it on the turn table. This was Ann's last night in Guadalajara. In the morning, her parents would be there to take her and Barbara away on a tour through Mexico. The arm was pushed back on the record player, and the same song played over and over. Ann knew she would never see Raùl again.

"I guess you're anxious to get home to Danny," Ann's parents said to her the next day when they were all standing admiring the large Orozco mural in the Governor's Palace. The mural showed Hidalgo bearing a flaming sword, dominating a host of dying men. At the right of the picture was a sinister murky world filled with Nazis and swastikas. "Not really," Ann said. "He only wrote me one letter the whole time I was here. He's a rat fink." Barbara was saying goodby to Juan. But it was not really goodby, of course. There was a possibility that she was engaged. Surely one summer soon she would return and they would be married. Outside of the Palace a black car was waiting to take them to the airport.

As they flew towards Acapulco, a well-dressed man of a certain age sitting on Ann's right was propositioning her. Barbara, sitting on her left, was throwing up into the little white bag. Ann did not bother to try to look out the window. She knew they were flying over the mountains forever.

That night she sat with her family in the cocktail lounge of the Hotel Mirador in Acapulco looking over the ravine. A man is climbing the rocks. He has reached an illuminated shrine where he kneels and prays. He turns and poises on the edge. And, with the blessing of the God of Jumping Off High Cliffs into Deep Water, he dives down, far down into the churning green.

A week later Ann and Barbara were sitting eating hamburgesas in the coffee shop of the Hotel Alameda in Mexico City. They were approached by two well-dressed darkly handsome Mexican men who invited them to the cocktail lounge where their parents allowed them to repair as it was, after all, right in the hotel, and these men were doctors, even if they were Mexican. As Ann sipped her Black Russian she looked beyond Sergio through the glass wall which separated them from the glowing rooftop swimming pool.

Since the next night was to be their last night in Mexico, Ann and Barbara's parents allowed them to go out with these two doctors from Juarez to a night club in another part of the city.

The night club was done up with the silken tents of a harem in Mexico. Low lights lit up a central chamber, and off of this central chamber were smaller rooms. Barbara stayed at the table with her date while Sergio led Ann through a Turkish arch to show her what one of these rooms was like. They were like dim candlelight and kissing, and then noticing that part of Sergio had gotten outside of his trousers. Ann took it in her hand. "If you are worried about getting pregnant," he said, "don't worry, Honey. I have been jerking off all day especially for that reason. I do not want to get you pregnant, Honey. Believe me. I am a gynecologist. I know what I'm doing. I have been jerking off all day, and believe me, the sperm are no good." Ann imagined him performing abortions. And then she forgot everything.

The fog rolls in through the Golden Gate covering the Bay

behind her as Ann climbs a hill in Berkeley carrying her books in front of her on her way back from the library to her room in the dorm. As she sets her books down on her desk she sees a blue airmail envelope. "Oh, Gawd," she says to her roommate. "This doctor I met in Mexico last summer has written to me."

Dearest honey:

I'm very happy for receive your letter you write very well the spanish only with the time and a little more experience you can do it very well. I hope you and your family are happy again in home and with all your friends, and special you work very hard and study well in the school—

I'm sending you this picture, because if your room is big you can "frighten the mice." I remember you very well and really I hope to see you one of these days don't worry I will dearest "thing." I want to see you again and please remember me I do very much. Say hello to your girl friends and give a big kiss from me and for you everything.

love as ever—
Sergio

The Psychology of Sex

ONE DAY when Ann was going up in the elevator to her room on the top floor of the dorm she saw these words pinned to the wall: *The Psychology of Sex*. There was a sign-up sheet and a pencil on a string. Glancing at the signatures she was surprised to see that Annette, the roommate they had stuck her with, had volunteered for this experiment. For Annette was an extremely religious person. She was a virgin.

Annette didn't know the first thing about sex. But she didn't approve. So Ann was surprised that she was volunteering for anything to do with sex. Ann herself was starting to wonder what it was all about. So she signed her own name.

Now she was walking through the labyrinthine institutional pink hallways of the psychology building to room sixty-nine. Now she was sitting across the table from a strange man. Other strange men were watching her through one-way mirrors.

"Now I want you to read from these cards out loud, one after another, flipping them up," the strange man said. There was a pile of cards face down on the table before her. Ann turned over the first card and cleared her throat.

"Tit."

The man gestured with his arm. She flipped to the second. "Clit."
The third was a verb: "Fuck."
She opened her mouth for the fourth: "Cock."
Then "Ding!"
Then "Dang!"
Then "Dong!"
At last Ann raised her eyes.
"All right," the strange man said, "You can pass on to the next stage."
Before her now she found a book with a plain cover. She was to open to the page that was marked. All she had to do was read aloud to the man what was there printed in black and white:

> Fortunately, the night air was fragrant and balmy, for Annabelle hadn't time to put on much in the way of clothing. For she was in flight from the white slave driver and his instruments of torture. So she was barefoot when she gained entrance to the hidden chambers of the magician. He was naked beneath his billowing robes. She could feel her tits tilt. His huge member rose like the moon throbbing brightly. She looked down on her now naked hips, surprised and delighted to see she was now fitted with a holster ready for his gun. She was a cowgirl riding for the sunset! Then she rode him, up and down, again and again. His huge presence moved inside of her, his wild smile widened her—

Ann looked up. The passage had broken off.
The man cleared his throat and began to speak. He was passing her on to the third stage. She adjusted herself in her chair and opened to the next place in the book.
"Anna was a girl like you or me," Ann read aloud to the strange man,

> only she lived on the veld. One day, she was sitting in her grass hut and she was overcome by an overwhelming desire for peanuts. The thought of peanuts drove her out of doors and over the path until she arrived at the hut of

Dajiki. It just so happened that Dajiki was roasting some peanuts inside. And so she came inside, and his happy smile played over her, and he played with her until she couldn't take it any more. She had to have some peanuts. And so he let her have them, one after another, and they were all hot. Dajiki's cock was in Anna's cunt, throbbing and pulsing, and

Ann looked up. The man was taking notes.

"All right," he intoned. "You have passed the screening. We couldn't admit just anybody to the group. We had to know if you'd be able to handle it. However, the group couldn't wait to find out about you. It's been going on all along in a neighboring room. Since they're already in session, nobody can be admitted. You will fall far, far behind if you don't know what's happened before the session next week. However, while they can't be disturbed, they can be overheard." Then he handed Ann a pair of one-way earphones. She plugged them in her ear. There was some fuzz, then a man's voice, speaking distinctly:

"As for the re-pro-duc-tive pro-cess-es, uhh . . ."

"The reproductive processes," a woman's voice repeated, thoughtfully.

"The reproductive processes of the amoeba . . ."

"The amoeba?"

"The amoeba—the amoeba, uh, is a one-celled animal, that, uh moves by, uh making continually changing protrusions of its, uh, body."

There was a pause, and then the woman's voice, asking:

"And it uh, uh, reproduces by uh. . ."

"It reproduces by uh, asexual reproduction," the man finally said.

"Well, that's all we have time for," the strange man said, pulling Ann's plug. "Now, if you'll just fill out this questionnaire—"

Ann stared at the questions:

Now that you have heard what the group is like do you still want to be in it?
Did you find the screening process rigorous?
How rigorous?
How much do you really want to be in the group?

As Ann walked back across campus she thought about what had just happened to her. She didn't know why she had been put through all those tests just to discuss the sex life of an amoeba. Then suddenly it dawned on her that, in reality, there wasn't any group! She had been plugged into a tape.

Suddenly, the experiment was clear. After all, the strange man (who, actually, looked like a typical Greek) had explained it to her before she was released: "This experiment," he had said, "is not really about sex. It is, rather, about rites of initiation. The theory that we are trying to prove is that if you have to go through a rigorous enough initiation to get into a group you will believe that the group is worth it whether it is or not." Ann felt cheated. She felt she had been used.

When she got back to her room there was Annette, cutting out cute pictures and putting them on the wall. "Oh God," Ann said, "I missed lunch."

"You know, Ann," Annette said, "you use such bad language that you don't even hear it when you take the Lord's name in vain."

"You know, Annette," Ann said, "you're missing out on most of the world's great literature by so censoring yourself." Ann picked up a book and began to read. She wondered if she should warn Annette about the experiment. Annette was scheduled for next week. The idea of Annette mouthing obscenities to a strange man amused Ann. Of course, for her, it would be a sin. Perhaps Ann shouldn't let her go through with it. But then again, how could it possibly make any difference? Annette couldn't in all conscience be embarrassed. You can't be embarrassed by what you don't understand. And Annette didn't understand the words. For her, it was meaningless.

A Modern Apartment

It was impersonal and it was dehumanizing. It wasn't supervision, it was regimentation. Always lining up and standing in line. Always having to eat at a certain time. All they served was starch and gravy. She was going crazy. She didn't have any privacy. She was trying to get her parents to see why she shouldn't go back to the dormitory.

But they were thinking of why she shouldn't move into an apartment. Then she explained to them that people wouldn't be using her apartment for immoral acts. Everyone would have apartments of their own. They wouldn't need hers. So they agreed—Ann could have an apartment if it met certain conditions.

This was the apartment which met the conditions. It was new and it was safe—there was an elevator and a fire escape. Each unit had two bedrooms and two bathrooms. Each had a dining room which looked at the dining room opposite. From the dining room where Ann was sitting she could see into the dining rooms on the floor above and the floor below. The ceilings of every dining room glittered, and the whole building stared at the tiny glowing swimming pool which it enclosed. No one was swimming. This living space was up to code.

And Ann wasn't living here alone. At first it had been going to be only her and Ellen, but Ann's parents hadn't thought that would be enough. So now Ann had three roommates. Ellen had dredged up two other girls, and Ann had explained to her parents what model roommates these three girls would be. Then Ann's father had set up a business meeting with the other fathers, and they had all signed the papers. So now they had a lease in the Zoo.

Ann looked across the wood-colored formica dining table at Melinda, one of the roommates Ellen had dredged up. The flowing sleeves of Melinda's leopardskin dressing gown were pushed back. In one hand she held a mirror, and in the other, a metal instrument clamped onto the eyelashes of one of her eyes. Then she exhaled, and switched eyes. Ann was in the middle of a physics experiment. In the dining room on the floor below somebody was already on to the next problem.

"Somebody's been eating my food," Ellen said looking in the refrigerator with her hand on her hip. "Somebody's been eating my food, too," Ann said, adjusting her pendulum for the x to the nth time. "It wasn't me," Melinda sniffled. They all knew it was Darlene, the roommate Melinda had dredged up as a fourth. But they couldn't prove it. Darlene was on a diet; they couldn't eat her food; she didn't have any in the refrigerator. Then Darlene herself burst in before Ann could get her calculations straight.

Not just Darlene herself, but her boyfriend and his boyfriend, and his boyfriend. Darlene was more than a roommate; she was a gang. Ann and Ellen were outnumbered. They hid in their room. But Darlene found them there.

"You still working on that experiment?" Darlene asked, opening Ann's closet. "You know, the trouble with you, Ann," Darlene said helpfully, "is that all your clothes are dark. There isn't a bright color in here." Ann looked with righteous indignation at her black turtleneck, her brown sweater, and her loden green coat hanging there in despair. Darlene was trying on her navy blue ski sweater.

"Barry's here!" Melinda called in a whisper as she passed down the hall faster than usual with her long brown hair piece coming loose. So Ann gave up and went out to the living room. Barry was large in the armchair. The room was thick with the scent of Canoe.

Canoe was the men's cologne worn most profusely by fraternity boys from the better houses. Barry was a fraternity boy from one of the better houses, and that was why he thought he was so great. That was why Ann thought he wasn't. To her, the Greeks had come to represent a system of false values. Clearly it was more in to be out. It pleased Ann that Barry must think he was slumming when he visited at her apartment. Anyway, that was how she felt when she visited at Barry's apartment. Because Barry was living in an apartment, an apartment in their building. He wasn't living in his fraternity house because he was too selfish.

He needed his own bedroom, he explained to Ann, showing it to her. She drank the drink he had mixed for her while he pushed off his shoes and stretched like an animal. He assumed his good looks were infallible. He assumed that they were going to screw.

He wasn't at all Ann's type. He was a business major. He wore suits when he went out on dates with sorority girls from the better houses who had to be in by a certain hour. Ann never went out on dates with Barry. That would have been socially unacceptable. No one knew they were here together alone now. They weren't talking.

Neither pretended beyond the bare minimum that they had anything to talk about together. Ann hadn't planned to be here screwing Barry again. Since she was drunk, she thought she could excuse herself later on the grounds that she was drunk.

In no time at all, she was back in her own apartment. Darlene's gang was crowding the living room. Melinda was displayed on the couch, comprehensively groomed. Ann reached her own room, and fell into the dark.

"Hunh?" Ellen said, waking up. "Did you get the solution to your physics problem?"

"Yes, but I had to cheat," Ann said, pulling off the clothes she had just pulled on. As she crawled into bed she could hear Ellen's quiet snoring across the room. Then she heard the strum, and the high pitch of Darlene's soprano piercing through the wall: "We shall overcome."

"We shall simply find another apartment," Ellen said the next morning peering into the empty refrigerator.

"We have simply found another apartment," Ann said when her parents phoned on Sunday. Then she explained to them that the apartment they had found was ideal—upstairs in an older building with a fireplace. She would have described the twining vines and sheltering brown shingles to them but all they were interested in was whether the building was a firetrap. It was impossible, actually, to show them just how an older building was less corrupt than a modern apartment. So she showed them a fait accompli. She would have to prove it to them.

And it wasn't long before she was able to write to them that she was now dating a very decent and sincere fellow named Edward. It was as if getting away from that plastic apartment had made it possible to have a real relationship.

To Edward, she was a real person. Edward belonged to a radical political party. One night, he took her to one of their parties. The room was dark. People sat on the floor with their backs to the wall passing a marijuana cigarette from hand to hand. Music filled the room. That night back at Edward's Ann stepped out of her blue work shirt and blue jeans and Edward stepped out of his. Then, defying the war raging outside in the world, they made love.

"Barry's been phoning you," Ellen said when Ann came in. The phone rang. "It's Barry again, for you."

Ann made a face. "Hello?"

"Hello, Ann, how do you like your new place?"

"Very much, thank you."

"It sounds just terrific. I'll have to see it to believe it."

He was coming over! Let him. Let him see for himself. She would show him. He wasn't going to get her to go back to the Zoo with him. He just wanted to show her his new car. She went for a ride with him in order to make it clear to him that his car meant nothing to her. He was just stopping by the Zoo to pick something up. Ann kept her coat on when she sat on the edge of Barry's couch and refused a drink. She was doing very well, she told Barry. She was doing very very well. She gave him a small political lecture and outlined a few theories of literature. He was genuinely interested, he told her, pushing off his shoes. So she told him she was now going with a man she was in love with, and he was in love with her. She showed herself to the door. No thanks, she would walk. What was a rather long walk home in the dark compared to the moral victory?

But one day when Ann was sitting on Edward's proletarian bed the phone rang suddenly right under her. Since she was right there, she answered it. It was Lois Davis, a friend of hers from high school. How nice! What a surprise! But Lois hadn't called to talk to her. Ann didn't know that Lois knew Edward. Wait—she had introduced them herself. How could she forget. She would run and get Edward for her. Here he was. She handed him the phone and discreetly left the room and stood behind the door. Edward was telling Lois that he had got the tickets dear and he couldn't wait either. There was something soppy about Edward. Something too childishly romantic. Only last week he had given her, Ann, a book of poetry which he couldn't really get into and he had inscribed it: "For Ann—love and splendor, Ed."

Ann started spending more time at home. Ellen's boyfriend Mike was always there, playing flamenco guitar on the floor. Ellen had borrowed Ann's blue pleated skirt and had worn it in a marshmallow fight she had had one night in front of the fire with Mike. She had said she would have it cleaned, but that was two weeks ago, and there it was, still on a chair.

Portland, Oregon

ANN WASN'T SOMEONE who had been jilted by her lover. She had not been betrayed by a friend. She wasn't an annoyance to her roommate, and she wasn't a disappointment to her parents while she was asleep. She was asleep. She was oversleeping. The dream on her screen had become so archetypically boring that she could see herself struggling to suspend disbelief. So she realized that she had woken up.

She was sorry. And sorry again when she saw that she was going to be late for creative writing class. So she yanked on her avant-garde white bellbottoms, strapped on her sandals of freedom, pulled a tee-shirt down over her lonely braless breasts, and looked for her proletarian green army jacket. Then she found a letter for her on the table, and glancing at the postmark, she headed for the door. Portland, Oregon.

Portland, Oregon! The very words were a bell tolling her back. Back over the years to the back seat of the family car. The car is moving across the West. It is on a family vacation. Now it enters a strange city, Portland, Oregon. This is not its destination. It's just getting gas here. Ann looks out the back window into the glare of gas station lights. Because of the glare, she can't see Portland,

Oregon. Instead, she realizes, she is seeing the same moment, several years later. She sees herself grown up into a woman. Herself in the driver's seat now. From the back seat, Ann sees herself in profile. To Portland, Oregon, she is a woman of infinite possibility. She has no past. Ann knows with a certainty that this will come to pass. If the Buick slides off to a motel now, it is no matter. She will be back here.

The letter was from Arthur, who was going to school at Reed, in Portland. He said it was raining, blah, blah. Half of the letter was in French. Bleh, bleh. There was crying in her heart like it rained on the town.

Everything was the same when she returned later that afternoon. What was this languor which penetrated her heart? Ellen came in bringing Mike, and Mike sat down on the floor and started picking on his flamenco guitar. They were so much in love. Ann went into the other room to give them the semblance of privacy.

She looked at the phone. Her soul was in torment. She dialed Greyhound.

It would only take fourteen hours to get to Portland. She would just go away, visit Arthur for the weekend. If he didn't mind having her. He couldn't refuse. She and Ellen always put him and his roommates up when they came down to Berkeley to see San Francisco. "I'll get you a bed in the women's dorm," he was saying into her receiver. There was no getting out of it now.

"That's wonderful," Ellen and Mike said, when she told them her resolution. Mike even offered to drive her to the station.

Now the bus was pulling away and Ann was blowing this burg. She was heading out, she was bound for the great Northwest. The man sitting next to her fell into the aisle. Anything might happen. Ann was on the road. They stopped at a station. Then they stopped at another. It seemed to be the same station. Then they stopped at another. It seemed to be the same station. Ann went to the cafeteria. Ann went to the lavatory. Nobody knew her name. Then it was night; the signs came on. She tried not to look tired. Arthur was there in the glare of bus station lights.

"Portland?" Arthur repeated, looking at her doubtfully. "Actually, we hardly ever go into Portland. The people of Portland are a bit hostile to us Reedies. But there is one thing you shouldn't miss while you're here."

"What's that?" Ann asked, getting into Arthur's car. "Is this a stick shift? I just learned how to drive with a stick. Thanks for coming for me so late. You must be tired. Why don't you let me drive?"

"I am tired," Arthur said. "But I'd better drive anyway. This isn't actually my car. Mine died last week."

"What did you say it was I shouldn't miss?" Ann asked.

"The flower gardens," Arthur said. "But I'm not sure if they're blooming now or not." Then he looked at Ann in that way he had. They had stopped at the signal.

It was as if more than a weekend had passed when Ann set foot back in Berkeley. Her final story was already overdue in creative writing. Now it was coming to her. She must hand it in late. She must call her professor to ask his permission. She didn't wish to be a bother. On the contrary, he sounded pleased to hear from her. But he wasn't going to be in his office. He wondered if it would be too much trouble for her to bring it by his place? Ann remembered what's-her-name and her birth control pills saying she was going up to the Avenue to look for this very professor. Now he was inviting her, Ann, to come to his house. "It won't be any trouble at all; it'll be easy," she answered him, naturally.

So Ann pulled on her avant-garde white bellbottoms, fresh from the laundry. And now, her sandals—they were getting a bit loose, and she'd always had trouble with that strap. Ellen dabbed her behind each ear with perfume. Mike let her drive. She walked up the steps. In her hands she held a great story. She had rung the bell. A woman answered, and Ann began to tell her her business. The woman took Ann's story out of her hands. In her arms she held the baby of domesticity. On her body she wore the apron of wedlock. It was a story about a flower that only blooms every hundred years. Over her shoulder, Ann could glimpse the professor of fiction reclining on his bed of roses. Then Mike drove her away into the night of predictable signs.

Return to the High Country

WHEN FATHER WAS A YOUNG MAN, before your mother hooked him, he went on the greatest adventure of his life, roughing it with the boys through the most spectacular scenery one could barely imagine—a pack trip in Glacier Park. And so he married your mother, and he had two boys of his own, only they weren't boys, they were girls. He just called them boys. "Hey, boys, c'mere and look at this chipmunk!" And every year as the little family was growing up Father took them on a family vacation. And they went to Yosemite, and they went to Lake Arrowhead, and they went to the Grand Canyon, and they went to Yellowstone, and they went to the Grand Tetons—that was indeed spectacular scenery, but it wasn't a pack trip in Glacier Park. And now the younger daughter had gone off to Berkeley, and the older daughter was looking for a husband, and your mother doesn't like the thought of riding on a mule. And so on the last day of this August we shall all meet in Yosemite, and we will set out at last together once more on a pack trip into the high country. Your mother will stay back at the Awannee.

Ann had a Cal sweatshirt inside out tied around her waist. She was wearing blue jeans and tennis shoes, and she pulled herself up confidently onto the back of her mule. Everyone in the expedition was mounting. Everyone but Barbara. Barbara wasn't getting on her mule because she knew it would kick her. She was just sneaking away behind it when Ann jumped down, and holding the reins of her own mule in one hand she gave Barbara a leg up with the other.

The ancient prospector, who knew this country like the back of his weathered hand, rode past on the lead mule, and Father, on his mule, was right behind. The other people in the party rode past. Ann had mounted again, but she held her mule in check, waiting for Barbara. Barbara's mule wouldn't move. "Kick it with your heels!" Ann suggested. "I am kicking it!" Barbara screamed, and her mule started to reel in circles and it was off. Ann followed immediately behind.

Because actually she couldn't stop her mule from running. The best thing to do was to think that she wanted it to run, and that she actually wasn't terrified of falling off. Because if a mule knows you're afraid it will take advantage of you, so you must never scream. Barbara was screaming that her mule wouldn't stop. Then it came up behind the last mule in the party and fell into line, walking. Ann's mule was walking now, too. "Walk!" she said. And hoof after hoof the mules walked surefootedly up the mountain and out of the valley. And as Ann looked back, way back beneath her—for she could look back easily now, now she was one with her saddle—she could feel the air clarifying, and the dark shadows of evening gather. But it wasn't evening. It was eleven o'clock in the morning. Ann untied her sweatshirt and pulled it on.

As they went up the mountain the air grew colder. Ann began to wish that she had brought her hat. The landscape to each side blurred into mist, and the mist then was rain. Ann's tennis shoes were soaking through. That was part of roughing it. This rain would pass and the sun would come out. They wouldn't *have* pack trips if the weather was going to be bad. It started to snow. Could this snow really be happening? These white flakes floating down through the dark? Ann's wet tennis shoes froze into ice. Was she going to lose a toe?

All the mules stopped. Everyone was getting down. Ann jumped down and stomped her feet. Barbara was calling, and Ann went over to help her down. Everyone was getting out their box lunches, which had been prepared back at the hotel. Barbara was asking Ann if she knew where the bathroom was. Apparently, there was no bathroom here. "You'll have to go behind a tree," Ann suggested. "Come with me and guard me," Barbara whispered. And so Ann and Barbara went behind a tree, and there Barbara told Ann that she had just unexpectedly gotten her period, and Ann said that people went on pack trips year after year, and nothing really happened that they had to worry about.

The snow was coming down in a thick blanket all around them when they set off again, as if they could never get to where they were going. But these trips into the wilderness are calculated to give you that feeling, and also to bring you at last safely into camp. They had come into camp.

Early in the morning Ann rose and found icicles hanging from the eaves of the tent. Real icicles! The cowboys were serving up mountains of authentic sourdough pancakes.

They rode out again, single file, tracking through the snow. Every so often, weights of snow would fall down from the high branches of the huge trees all around them. Ann wondered how the ancient prospector could find the way through these trees. It all looked alike to her.

They were coming down a steep ravine now. So this was the way. Swift tracks of rabbit and deer were clear in the snow. *They* had known where they were going. Ann saw a stream opening in the snow. She would never have guessed it was there. Now they were crossing this same stream again. Or did it just seem that way to Ann?

Now it seemed like they were going up the same hill again. And now they were in a dense wood. Barbara was screaming. Her mule was going round and round. She couldn't control it. Ann was embarrassed. In front of the ancient prospector! The ancient prospector was about to speak.

He said that he was lost. They would have to go back the way they came. And they did. And then the ancient prospector led them a few hundred yards over the rise of a little hill and there was the road. Then someone came to take their mules away, and a van came to drive them back down into the valley as the snow started to come down again.

Daddy and the boys couldn't get into the Awannee without a

reservation, but there was no reason why Mother should give up her comfortable room there. Daddy and the boys could rent a tent in Camp Curry. They were too dirty to go to the Awannee anyway.

Daddy couldn't even go there for dinner—he didn't have a tie. He and the boys ate at the cafeteria and bedded down early. As Ann lay awake in her cot she thought she saw shadows moving across the face of the tent. Or was the door of the tent flapping?

In the morning they learned that a bear had been in the camp during the night. He had gone into a tent and had taken a Monopoly game out. He had thought that there would be food in the package. When he found out there wasn't, he smashed it on a rock.

Squaw Valley

As they walked through the lobby of the Student Union Jimmy pulled Ann to the wall where there was a bulletin board. This was a bulletin board which Ann never checked. It never had anything to do with her. It was on a wall by the door which she was always walking out of or in through on her way to Pauley Ballroom for a dance or a political meeting, or on her way through to the big easy chairs and couches of Heller Lounge to study, or on her way down to the Bear's Lair for a hamburger and a juke-box and black kids playing cards by day, or by night for a cabaret. Only once before had she actually stood by this bulletin board—she had stood with the other people who had just come in the door while they had all listened to the news coming out of the speakers which usually played music that Kennedy had been shot, the announcement of the end of the world at last. That was before acid. That was before she went everywhere with Jimmy.

Technically, Ann had known Jimmy ever since grammar school. But all she remembered of Jimmy from grammar school was the terrible shock she had felt one day in the last half of the eighth grade when she saw him walking his bike so that he could walk Carol Kaufman home from school. The terrible shock that Carol Kaufman was going steady. The terrible realization that Carol

Kaufman had changed in the last half of the eighth grade from Carol Kaufman to a big thing that wore flats and went steady.

In high school Ann was vaguely aware that Carol Kaufman had stopped going steady with Jimmy, had grown taller with a hugely long skirt, and had started to go steady with an even taller thing with a crew cut. That is all Ann can remember about Carol Kaufman, or whoever she was, in high school. The only thing Ann can remember about Jimmy from high school was that she had known that he skied, because Arthur always went skiiing with him.

When she had learned that, she had assumed that Jimmy had read *La Nausée*, could recite "Sailing to Byzantium," and even had a special interest in Byzantine art. So when she and Arthur were talking over who they would invite to their Quatorze Juillet party during French class Ann had suggested Jimmy. A crapaud de dégoût look came into Arthur's face. This was the same expression Arthur had for Danny with whom he also skied. "But you always go skiiing with him!" Ann said. "Yes, but only because he's good to go skiiing with," Arthur said, and that was the end of it.

So when Ann ran into Jimmy when she was moving into a dorm in Berkeley and Jimmy was moving into the men's dorm opposite they greeted each other as old friends. Jimmy suggested to her that she take a philosophy course, and she didn't see him again for two years.

It was quite a coincidence when she ran into him again. Ann was moving again—from one apartment into another. Ellen had found an apartment with Mike. Jimmy had just moved into an apartment over a bookstore. To get to the stairs that led up to it you had to go through a black door that had once been painted green. This door had, indeed, once been the green door of the song "Green Door." Ann had always resented this song for keeping her out of the secret it was hiding. Now Jimmy had moved behind the green door, and he could help her and her roommate Faith move into their apartment.

Ann was lucky to run into such an old dear friend as Jimmy— someone she could relax with, someone she could be herself with. She had been having a discouraging time of it lately. Every man she met only wanted to fuck on the first date. No one seemed to want to bother to be her friend first, so she had nearly resigned herself to a life of loneliness, she told Jimmy. Now she would have companionship while she was waiting for a real relationship to come along.

Ann's father had allowed her to rent this apartment on the condition that she and her roommates got a new refrigerator for it. Only then would it be up to code. Ann and Faith had driven up from L.A. in Faith's car, and Charity wouldn't be there for a week, so Ann and Faith had to find a refrigerator by themselves. Then Ann's friend Jimmy offered to help them. It was easy with Jimmy helping them. He found them one for $15.00. "It was easy," he said. It was, if anything, not as good as the one Ann's father had condemned, but it was another refrigerator, and that was all they needed.

After they got the refrigerator in, Ann and Faith decided to get a kitten. Charity wouldn't be there for two days. Charity hadn't helped them get the refrigerator. And since Charity wasn't there she couldn't tell them that she was allergic to cat hair. Jimmy came over to see it as soon as they got it.

He could make the cat work in any position. Ann had not known this before about cats. Pretty soon, Ann was spending all her time with Jimmy.

Now Jimmy was pointing to the notice on the bulletin board. It was announcing the Cal Winter Ski Holiday at Squaw Valley.

That was easy; Ann didn't ski. She was surprised that Jimmy would think that she'd be interested. It was impossible. She didn't have any ski pants. She could rent them! But that was the kind of thing all the sorority and fraternity idiots went to. That was easy, they could say they were married and get their own room. That appealed to Ann, the make-believe part, and they went over to the counter and bought their tickets.

Just like that. That was how Ann and Jimmy did things. Like the time Jimmy arrived on Ann's doorstep and invited her to go for a motor-scooter ride just like that when she knew he didn't have a motor-scooter. And they had ridden high up in the hills to Tilden Park, where you're not supposed to go at night. And they had come to the dark silent merry-go-round where it looked like they couldn't get in, all the canvas was tied down. But Jimmy lifted up the bottom of the canvas and they were in, just like that. Without making any noise, they crept up and sat on the dark horses.

On the way out of the park they ran out of gas. Easy. It was all downhill. They could coast, and when they got to the flats, there would be a gas station. And so they coasted in the rush of the night, they coasted in the dark, in the silvery street-light, until they stopped. They had stopped on the flat part of Oxford Street still several blocks from the gas station. The other problem was that neither of them had any money on them.

Ann waited on the sidewalk behind a bush while Jimmy went up to the one house that had lights on and knocked on the door. The porchlight went on. Dogs started to bark. The door opened. Ann waited. Then just like that Jimmy was back with forty-two cents. "It was easy," he said. And together they walked the bike to the gas station.

They went everywhere together after that. Ann never knew what Jimmy would come up with next. One day she came home from school and saw him standing by an old car parked in front of her house. When she got closer she saw that he was painting. He was just putting the finishing touches on a bat. "Would you like to take a spin in my bat-mobile?" he asked her. He had bought an old car and turned it into a bat-mobile. Just like that.

Now that they had a bat-mobile they could drive over to what's-his-name's house and pick up a lid of grass. They were just about to run out of grass. Now they had a bat-mobile just in time. Dick and Harry, who lived at Jimmy's house, said they'd come, too.

They went by night. Dick went into the house to get the stuff. Riding in the bat-mobile was the height of luxury. Sirens and lights made them pull over.

They were asked to get out of the car. Ann couldn't believe it. How had they known they were carrying dope? Later Jimmy explained it—the police were resentful that they were driving a bat-mobile instead of a normal American car, and were hoping to catch them with bats in their car. Ann watched while the police shone their flashlights all over inside the car—in the front seat and the back seat. Jimmy stepped up to them. "Wouldn't you like to look in the trunk?" he invited. Ann watched with horror while Jimmy unlocked the trunk. The policemen looked in the trunk, then they all got back in the police car and drove away. Ann couldn't believe their luck in getting the dope to disappear in thin air just when they needed it to. Then Jimmy produced the lid from his pocket. It was all done by magic.

Magic allowed for anything to happen. With magic Ann could write a story for her creative writing class. They were over at Jimmy's the night before it was due. Jimmy put on a record and Ann lit up a joint. Then Jimmy sat down and read to Ann from the newspaper. "Have you ever considered committing suicide?" he read. It was the Question Man in the paper. It was the answer. Ann picked up a pen and wrote "Have you ever considered committing suicide?" Then she wrote the story of the asking of that question. "The answer to a question is a question," she told Jimmy. "Why do you ask?" he asked.

When Jimmy walked into her house one day with a big regal super-spade Ann didn't ask where he had got him. Super Spade made them all feel quite at home right away. Faith was doing her zoology, and Charity was knitting and burning her split ends off one by one with her cigarette butt. Jimmy was playing with the cat on the floor—getting a cat's-eye view of things. Super Spade had some really fine dope, and after he had passed it around he began to tell them all the story of Lot's wife. He played all the parts himself—all the wicked people, God, and Lot, and finally at the end he was Lot's wife turning around and turning into a pillar of salt with his powerful index finger pointing at Ann. "You, Baby, are jes' like Lot's wife," he told Ann.

That night, Ann told Jimmy that she had thought it over, and she was willing to try this LSD he had been telling her about. He had told her that words couldn't describe it.

Later, when she tried to describe the experience to Faith, all she could tell her was that everything is everything, that there are colors in the world which we do not allow ourselves to see in everyday life that are of the most exquisite beauty. She could not describe them to Faith, because they had no names. They did not belong to the naming world. Ann tried to describe these colors by playing Brahms' violin concerto on the record player. "Listen! Listen!" she pleaded, but it was no use. A record player was a ridiculous machine. She couldn't explain to Faith that she had seen the truth.

It was a secret between her and Jimmy. Just the secret of the universe, that's all. The thing about a secret is that it's so good you want to give it away. Ann found when she ran into Ben, her creative writing teacher, that she was trying to give it to *him*, all in a hurry. But what was the use? It would take more than a lifetime to describe. And it was obvious that she was only going to be talking with him here, on the steps of the Student Union, for a few minutes. She had just run into him. She hardly knew him. He was on his way somewhere, and she was on her way to meet Jimmy.

Jimmy was waiting for her at the fountain. He was wearing his friendly magician's smile. Ann wondered why Arthur had not seen in Jimmy what was obviously there, beaming out. Could Jimmy have changed that much since high school? Perhaps she had been wrong about Arthur. Now, at the fountain, Jimmy was handing her three pennies. She threw them, six times. Ah, and each time she threw them Jimmy made a mark. One below the other, in the order that the heads and tails combined each time. And when they were done they had made a hexagram. And they opened to the first page of the book and looked up the hexagram in a chart of all possible hexagrams, and the hexagram had a number. Ah, then they leafed through the book until they came upon the number. Over the number was a hexagram, and under them was a story. Pennies did the trick, although it would have been better with yarrow sticks. But they didn't know where to get hold of any yarrow sticks. Jimmy had borrowed the *I Ching*.

When they got back to Ann's house, Super Spade was there. Faith had her shoes off and was studying her zoology. Charity was knitting and burning off her split ends one by one with her cigarette butt. Jimmy got down on the floor and started "seeing things from a cat's point of view." Super Spade rolled up a big number and they passed it around. Jimmy said, "Oh, *I* see, cats are really conscious of changes in temperature. When you're down on the floor you can feel a vast difference in temperature from your head to your toes." "The cat's only on the floor because I pushed it off the couch," Charity said, but the rest of them got down on the floor to try it. "See what I mean?" Jimmy said. "Yeah, it sort of tingles," Faith said.

One by one they all got back into chairs, and Super Spade started to tell them a story. It was the story of Samson and Delilah. Super Spade was big powerful Samson strutting nobly in the living room with rippling muscles and electric hair. He was all the puny Philistines, looking at this big dude and trying to find some way to bring down his temple. And he came, as Delilah, all sin and treachery and lechery. As Delilah he was absolutely irresistible.

It was all silent after the story. "Well, Baby, it's time for me to split," Super Spade said, getting up gracefully. "Time for me to cut out, too," Jimmy said, and Ann walked them to the door. Then, as Charity and her boyfriend were going to screw in Charity's bedroom which was the living room, Ann and Faith went upstairs with the cat to Faith's room to study.

They had started in to study when they realized they were listening to the thumping coming from downstairs. "This happens every night," Faith said. "It's hard to study." "Well, we can't very well stop them," Ann said. "What is it like?" Faith asked Ann. Faith was a virgin. "Well, words can't really describe it," Ann said. "Like acid?" Faith asked. "Well, sort of, not really, I don't know." "Do you and Jimmy screw?" Faith asked. "Well, actually, we don't yet," Ann said. They would eventually. In the natural course of things. There was no reason not to.

But the next night Jimmy came over with his old friend Lyle who had just rolled into town. He had just gotten out of prison. He was a great guy. They were both proposing gallantly to accompany Ann to the rally in the park.

It was dark when they got to the park. Most of the opening speeches were over. It was that point in the rally when it was time to take action. Long hairs were milling back and forth in the crowd of long hairs, when suddenly the crowd began to yell from the center. It turned and started running towards Ann, and every which way out. Ann heard the thumping noises and saw the crowd running towards her. Then suddenly everything came pouring out of Ann's eyes and throat and ears, and she was running, past people holding their faces and holding their bellies. The Philistines were throwing tear-gas. Ann was crying as if her heart would break. She looked up through her tears into Jimmy's face, to see that he was weeping, too. But he turned her gaze to Lyle, so that she could see that Lyle was also crying.

When Ann said goodnight to Jimmy on her doorstep, she wondered if he would kiss her goodnight. She lingered on the doorstep to give him an opportunity, and he was not blind to the opportunity. He kissed her goodnight. And then Lyle kissed her goodnight also.

After that, they went everywhere together. Jimmy always kissed her goodnight now, and Lyle always kissed her goodnight, too. Then she would shut the door and race upstairs to the bathroom to wash her mouth. She didn't know how much longer she could stand being kissed by Lyle.

And now another old friend of Jimmy's had joined them. Mose was an incredible person. He went on acid trips without acid. He had never tried acid. He was naturally stoned. His family had tried to have him locked up. They had said he was dangerous. Dangerous! Can you imagine? Jimmy had testified at his sanity trial. Jimmy was his hero. Mose was forty-five. He had tried to push a girl out a window. He would do anything for Jimmy. He would lend Jimmy his apartment for the day so Ann and Jimmy could take acid there. Jimmy told Ann that Mose's place had a lot of vibes.

It had linoleum on the floor. Ann thought that if she wanted to take off all her clothes when the acid came on—it wasn't like that, of course. It was acid, and there was no way to really remember it or think about it when she was not on it, when she was in the other room which stands for it. Ann looked up into Jimmy's face and saw mask after mask peel away there. He was a prince. He was a boy. He was a monster.

Since Lyle had been able to join Ann and Jimmy on their acid trip he was there to walk Ann home with Jimmy. Ann didn't linger on the doorstep. She was tired. What was the use?

When she came in Rhett was lying on her bed. Rhett was one of the sexiest-looking people Ann had ever seen. He was in her creative writing class. Although Ann did not see him that often, there was a special bond between them. Ann did not see Rhett too often because he was a meth freak, and when he was on methadrine he was always speeding around. But when he was coming off of speed he would sometimes come over to Ann's to sleep. He was exhausted.

Ann asked Rhett to describe to her what methadrine was like. "I can't really put it into words," he said. "It's the only real substitute for sex I know." Ann wished that Rhett didn't take methadrine. "Doesn't anybody fuck anymore?" Ann asked Rhett. "Doesn't anybody fuck anymore?" she asked again, a little louder. Faith came and stood in the doorway. "Doesn't anybody fuck anymore?" Ann asked loudly, jumping up and down on the bed. Rhett jumped up and down on the bed shouting "Doesn't anybody fuck anymore?" too, and then he fell asleep.

Someday everything would be different. Ann and Jimmy would go away together to an uninhabited, unexplored, and undiscovered island. Together they pored over chart after chart in books of islands taken out of the library, looking for an island to discover. When they discovered it, they would go there. And they would live on fish and fruit, and they would find a waterfall and even have a little generator if they wanted to. "Yes," Lyle said, "we could bring seeds with us and grow whatever we pleased," and "Yes," Tom, Dick, and Harry said, "we could bring our stereo and run it on the generator." Ann wondered if she would spend all her time on the island trying to get rid of Lyle, Mose, Tom, Dick, and Harry. She had to go home to pack. She was leaving for Beverly Hills for Christmas vacation tomorrow.

At home, Ann's father took her aside to give her a serious warning. He had heard about some drug called LSD. He had heard it was dangerous. He had heard that it led to taking marijuana. He wanted to warn her. She thanked him for the warning. She had not known that about LSD.

Ann was allowed to go out for New Year's Eve. In fact, if she didn't go out for New Year's Eve she was supposed to be a social disaster. Ann knew that Barbara considered herself a social disaster in the eyes of the world because she didn't have a date for New Year's Eve this year. Barbara was acting like New Year's Eve really meant something, but Ann knew it wasn't any different from any other night. She and Jimmy probably wouldn't even go anywhere. They would probably just sit around his mother's house, where he was staying for Christmas vacation. Barbara seemed to think that Ann thought she was pretty hot having a date for New Year's Eve, but Barbara knew what kind of a person she really was. She knew that Ann performed disgusting and evil acts while she was supposed to be going to college at Berkeley.

"You do, don't you?" she asked Ann, getting into her flannel nightgown and preparing to go to bed at six o'clock because it was New Year's Eve and she didn't have a date. "What do you mean?" Ann asked. She hadn't told Barbara anything. It was true that one day while Barbara was putting on her eye make-up in front of the mirror she had said to Ann "Why don't you ever confide in me?

Why won't you be a real sister to me?" Ann had decided right then to give Barbara a little confidence to keep her from asking any more questions, but she hadn't actually told her anything incriminating, had she?

The door bell rang. Jimmy was in the living room, talking with her parents. Ann went out to the living room with her purse. Barbara came down the hall after her in her bathrobe. Surely she wasn't going to see them off? "And what are you *really* going to *do* tonight?" Barbara asked Ann in front of her parents. "I don't know what you're talking about, Barb," Ann said, in front of her parents.

Then she invited Barbara to come with her and Jimmy over to Jimmy's mother's house. She invited Barbara to come before anybody could say anything further, and Jimmy seconded the motion. He could think of nobody nicer to spend New Year's Eve with than Barbara. This made Barbara go and get dressed. Then the three of them went over to Jimmy's house to wait till it was over.

Ann had a Christmas present to give to Jimmy. It was the perfect gift for him. She had been so pleased when she had thought of it—it was an *I Ching*. And it was the best translation, the one with an introduction by Jung. She had been careful not to get him the wrong translation. When she handed it to him on New Year's Eve, and he held it in his hands and could tell that it was a large book under its Christmas wrapping, a smile came over his face. Then he handed Ann her present. She could tell by its size and heft that it was an *I Ching* under its Christmas wrappings, too. Did this spoil her surprise for him and his surprise for her or did it make it better? They both tore the paper away. They both had given each other *I Chings* for Christmas! They were both on the same wavelength. Ann looked at hers and smiled. It was the wrong translation.

Lyle, Tom, Dick, Harry, and Mose were there to welcome them when they got back to Berkeley. Ann should have been glad to see them. Wasn't everybody everbody? If Ann took acid with Lyle, Tom, Dick, Harry, and Jimmy she would find out. Faith decided to take it with them, too.

And so they all did it together. They dropped all together in the living room, on a sunny day. After a while, Ann realized she could go into her room where the light was better. She went in and sat down at her desk and looked out the window. There was no one else in there. In the middle, she walked out, and passed through the living room where Lyle, Jimmy, Tom, Dick and Harry were in various aspects, and she went up the stairs towards where the light was pouring from the window on the landing. From there she saw Faith sitting on the bed in her room. She came into Faith's room, and sat down in her rocker. The cat was sitting on the desk. Faith had been looking into the cat. Ann turned and looked into the cat. And so Ann and Faith saw the cat.

Later, when they had come down, Faith told the others that she and Ann had seen the cat. Then Dick told Faith what he had seen, and after that Dick stopped going everywhere with Lyle, Jimmy, Mose, Tom, and Harry, and started going everywhere with Faith. Faith and Dick were sleeping together now. Now Faith was into the secret.

Now Ann's resentment of Lyle, Mose, Tom, Dick and Harry was simply a paranoid hang-up, she realized when Jimmy proposed to her that they go to Squaw Valley for winter holiday as a married couple.

Now what Ann had wanted to happen all along, what she had expected to happen, was going to happen. Nonetheless, she was unprepared. She had no decent nightgown. Jimmy took her around to rent her ski equipment. He didn't know it, but it was a minor part of the preparation she had to do. She had to go shopping for a nightgown—by herself, in secret. She had to select the perfect nightgown. It wasn't this black negligée—the saleslady needn't make assumptions about her. Shorty pajamas were to be eliminated, flannel nightgowns needn't apply. If what was left was the perfect nightgown it was this white cotton one. It wasn't long, but it wasn't short. It wasn't see-through, but it was sleeveless. "Please tell me it's right," Ann asked Faith, when she had bought it and brought it home and tried it on in the afternoon. "It's really neat," Faith said. "It could pass as a dress."

When Jimmy came for Ann in the morning in the bat-mobile he did not know that the white nightgown was packed in Ann's bag. They were driving up to Squaw Valley in the bat-mobile alone. They weren't going on the bus with the fraternity boys and sorority girls.

Ann realized that she had never really seen Jimmy before until she saw him skiiing. Jimmy on skis was freedom itself, the easiest thing in the world. How light and swift he was, sailing on the mountain far away, and then there he was bending before her, helping her to put on her skis. And sweetly he led her to the beginners' class. And then he slid away, farther and farther away, and now, from very far away, he was waving to her, and she waved back.

Ann fell down in the snow. Why did Ann fall down in the snow? She fell down in the snow because she had neglected to realize that skis can cross in the back as well as in the front. She made a mental note to remember to consider what was behind her in the future. Now she would just lie here patiently in the snow until she figured out how to get up. For there was no need to hurry. She wearing ski pants, tights, two pairs of sox, two shirts, a sweater, a wooly hat, sunglasses, and gloves.

The instructor helped her up, and led her to a little hill that she was supposed to go down. But actually, she realized, she did not want to go down the little hill. Possibly she could learn just as much by looking. It was possible that if she looked very closely it would be better than actually having the experience. Ann had always believed in this sort of thing. She knew it was just a matter of belief. And then there was the argument which asked what was the point of picking yourself up out of the snow when you would just have to do it again in a minute?

Ann and Jimmy giggled about it at dinner. Jimmy had made her bring her pillow to sit on. And he had brought his pillow, and there they were in the dining hall with their pillows. As if they had snuck downstairs to be with the grown-ups and brought their pillows. The grown-ups were fraternity and sorority people who had no pillows. After dinner, while the grown-ups were still standing around, Ann and Jimmy crept over to the huge stone fireplace, and sat down on their pillows in front of it. Pretty soon, all the grown-ups started to sit down on the floor behind them. There was to be a concert, and Ann and Jimmy were to be allowed to stay up for it. Then the Lovin' Spoonful appeared and set up their equipment in front of the fireplace. And when they sang "Do You Believe in Magic?" they were playing it for Ann and Jimmy only. Because as everybody knows, grown-ups don't believe in magic.

They couldn't stay for the party that went on afterwards, and yawning and hugging their pillows they dragged themselves heav-

ily upstairs to the room where, no matter how tired you are, there will always be a bit of hi-jinx brushing teeth, spattering each other, and showing each other mouths full of foaming toothpaste. And when at last Ann was in her white nightgown and under the covers they told each other goodnight, one after the other in answer to each other, until sleep spread across the room keeping them safe from the knowledge of who said goodnight last.

On the second day Ann did not remember how to put on her skis. She had to squat and pull off her gloves with her teeth, and pull on her gloves after and get up again. Today Ann was to go up in the chair lift. She was never afraid that the lift would break half-way up. If the lift stopped half-way up Ann would just sit in her chair. She was not afraid to sit in a chair. The trouble was, people kept coming up behind her. Ann could not remember which direction she was supposed to fall.

Then, in the afternoon, Jimmy took her on the best lift of all—the gondola. They didn't bring their skis. The gondola was really a neat ride. It was like the space bubble ride at Pacific Ocean Park.

At the top of the mountain was a chalet. It was a little cafe, where they could get steaming hot chocolate. It was like a little chalet in the Alps. Maybe, someday, Ann and Jimmy would be high in the Alps.

That night, Ann stood alone on the porch in the dark with couples who were standing together in the dark. She wondered what they thought of her. Did they think she was here alone by herself in Squaw Valley for the Winter Holiday? She took off her sapphire ring and put it on her marriage finger and turned it around so that the stone was inside and all that showed was the plain gold band. And Ann watched the skiers holding lighted candles, weaving in and out of the trees in the dark beyond the dark porch where she stood with the other people. She could not distinguish Jimmy from the other skiers.

Now Jimmy was back from the slalom. At last he had his skis off. It was time for bed. Jimmy's eyes sparkled. He was excited. He had a great idea. They would go ice skating.

Happy Valley

RHETT ARRIVED for Ann wrapped in his bedspread. He was escorting her to their creative writing final. He reminded Ann of their pact—*she* was to wear *her* bedspread. His was madras. There wasn't going to be a real final in creative writing. Hers was an American flag. Luckily, there weren't many people in the plaza as she crossed it in her strange toga. "What a beautiful dress!" "You should be arrested!" people said. Her creative writing teacher, however, didn't appear to notice what she was wearing.

Back in her uniform—a used black velvet jacket with padded shoulders—on Telegraph Avenue, she is walking home with Faith, who is being walked home by Dick, when suddenly this same teacher, Ben, appears before her, motioning the other way.

"Viennese Expressionist art, string quintet, free food," he says, breathless. Ann, Faith, Dick. He's telling them all about the opening at the art museum.

So they all follow him, through the dark, back to the museum. Faith and Dick lag behind. Or do Ann and Ben walk ahead? Does he choose her to walk with over them? Of course, he's never seen them before, and she's been his student for years. On her last story he had written, "I wish I had written this." And he had signed it—"Ben." But there's no reason to read anything into *this*. He's got a wife and baby. Ann clears her throat. "How is your little baby?" she says.

"Fine," he answers. "His mother just picked him up. I had him overnight at my house last night." Does this mean that his marriage has broken up? Is he trying to tell her that he's free? Ann thinks that's what he's saying. But she might have heard him wrong. Or only let herself hear what she wanted to hear. The door to the museum swings open.

It appears that the string quintet has finished playing, the food is all gone, and they have missed it. Ann and Ben walk around in the Viennese Expressionism anyway. They discover that Viennese Expressionism happens to be a favorite of each. Indeed, Ann has never liked Viennese Expressionism so well. But then Ben disappears.

Now several days later Ann sits at the fountain. It's time to meet Jimmy at the repair shop where her record player is being worked on. It had recently come out, as inevitably it would, that Jimmy had surreptitiously taken Ann's record player and had bored a small hole in it. His plan had been to install headphones. It was to be a surprise for her, and now it was broken. And now he didn't want to give her surprises anymore. She would rather he wouldn't. This was strictly business. She is about to go when Ben steps up and sits down beside her.

"I hope I'm not keeping you from meeting anyone," he says. Does he mean to point out to her that they have the appearance of sitting purposefully together? "Oh, no," she says. She can't tell him that she would rather be sitting here with him than going anywhere with another, despite the fact that she has to go meet Jimmy. Her record player is unfortunately broken.

It was a few days later when Ann was eating her lunch alone on the Terrace where, if you sit long enough, everyone in the University will go by, when Ben caught her eye. Then he was asking her to eat her lunch with him, but when she got to his table she saw he was sitting with two other men. They were all talking about how lucky they were to run into each other. Why didn't they get together more? Each protested that he didn't want to leave and go to class. It was almost too late. It was over too quickly. So they promised each other to meet each other at noon next Thursday at the Venez Expresso Cafe.

The question was, was Ann included in the invitation or not? Faith said she might as well go and find out.

Ben's friends stood up as she walked into the Venez Expresso in her see-through dress with just-visible bloomers. One got her chair. But Ben wasn't there. She looked up to see him just coming through the door. Then the conversation was fascinating as before. Before she knew it the waiter was recommending the sherbet, then suddenly it was time to leave, and they were agreeing to meet just the same in a week. Ann waited for Ben to disappear.

But apparently he was walking her way. In the nick of time they had discovered that Schubert was a favorite of each.

Ann's record player is fixed. She has a perfect Schubert string quintet to offer to play for Ben. Her place is only half a block away, not really out of Ben's way, wherever that lies.

As she flipped the switch that worked as if by a miracle that unlocked the music he stretched back on her flag. He put his hands behind his head and closed his eyes, totally absorbed in the music. Ann sat very quitely in the only chair in the room so as not to distract him. Since she had only one chair it didn't really mean anything that he was lying on her bed. They couldn't sit in the living room; Charity was asleep in there. Ben opened his eyes as the music finished, and then he was gone. The machine switched itself off.

Ann asked Faith if she should consider herself invited to the next Thursday lunch at the Venez Expresso so that Faith would tell her to go.

Ben's friends stood up as she walked into the Venez Expresso in her pin-striped and polka-dot suit. Their conversation was exceptionally amusing, especially after Ben joined them. Then they all laughed until it was time to go. It seemed that Ben was ready for some more Schubert. He loved Schubert so, and he didn't have a record player of his own. Once again, Ann brought him home.

Once again, Ben was stretched out on her bed. This time Ann perches on the edge of the bed to show him that he is welcome to the only chair. The music stops. She is looking into Ben's eyes. His eyes are bluer than any eyes she has ever seen before.

"Your eyes are so blue," she can't help saying.

"So blue and so cold," he says, sliding one warm hand inside her polka-dot collar. It slips inside her bra and encloses one of her breasts. It's warm. His mouth, his chest, the hairs curling up from the top of his shirt, his hands, everywhere, underneath her skirt between the gap in her black net stockings and the suspants she is wearing to hold them up. She wishes she could apologize for these contraptions—she has found the lump in his pants, incredulous and triumphant that this is happening, afraid that it will stop—he's already stayed longer than last time. Faith or Charity might interrupt it at any moment trying to get to the bathroom.

"I have to go," Ben says.

Ann looks askance at his shoes.

"I've promised these people who are letting me stay in their basement that I'd babysit for them tonight. Why don't you come back there for dinner? It's rather far. You like to walk?" Ben asks.

She loved to walk. She adored walking. There was nothing she'd rather do than walk. "Sure," she said.

It was an even longer walk than she had imagined. The sun was going down. It would be a very long walk back alone in the dark after dinner. She couldn't worry about that now. "This is the top of the hill," Ben assured her.

And now they walked on, gradually descending, by stone walls, past pillars, on crooked sidewalks, through a landscape which grew increasingly more lush. Tall fronds and overhanging branches brushed Ann's cheek as they walked past cascading gardens down a secret staircase between two roads. This was a side of Berkeley Ann had never seen before.

"Are we really still in Berkeley?" she asked.

"I call it Happy Valley," Ben confided, and he led Ann down the path at the edge of the house to a small door at the top of the back garden.

"This is an illegal apartment," he was telling her, fooling with an electric frying pan. Dinner was remarkable. They pushed back their chairs. Ann thought Ben was going to walk her home then, but he led her upstairs.

They were now in the downstairs of the house, on the front cover of *Family Circle*. "They'll be back at ten," Ben tiptoed. "The kids are asleep. Let's see what's on t.v." Of course, he couldn't very well take her home when he was supposed to be babysitting. She had until ten to be here with Ben. So they sat in front of the t.v. and held each other's knees. The movie they were watching was *L'Aventura*, where the point seems to be the search for the lost girl, and it turns out it isn't.

"I can hear them coming!" Ben said, bustling Ann downstairs where she could hear what must have been the father's heavy tread on the floor above her.

Ann could have had her jacket on to show Ben she was ready to be taken home when he came back downstairs. But she didn't want to bring the subject up. Still, she had to talk about something, so she asked Ben if he had ever performed Boku-maru. Boku-maru was a game she and Jimmy used to play. They had read about it in a novel. You get down on the floor with your legs spread opposite each other and press the soles of your feet to the soles of the feet of the other. It was a way of touching soles. Ann hoped Ben wouldn't think it was too corny. He said he'd like to try it. He had never done it. They undress from the ankle down. Their soles touch—they are touching all over! Ann's clothes are torn from her. Ben is naked, flying towards her.

"My wife hasn't slept with me for months. She never understood me. It was as if I were asleep. Then, one day, I woke up. And saw that I had to leave. But now, these past few days, under your flag, here in your bed, my arms around you, is eternity. It is as if I've always known you, as if we've loved each other all our lives," Ben said.

Ann had to agree. This was too good to be true.

Aspen, Colorado

WHEN ANN GOT THE NEWS that she was accepted at the Aspen Writers' Workshop she did a little tap dance for Faith in the kitchen. She did it to the tune of "I'm on my way to Os-lo, where I'll win the No-bel Prize. See all my friends in old Os-lo, etc." Of course she knew that the Nobel Prize wasn't given out in Norway, but now she had an excuse to get out of the L.A. smog for part of the summer. Actually, she wanted to spend the summer in Berkeley, but that was unrealistic. She couldn't very well tell her parents that she would rather be in Berkeley with Ben than in Beverly Hills with them, now could she? They would point out that school was out for the summer. They would point out that Berkeley was full of communists and drugs. Could this be a place that a girl from Beverly Hills could think of as home? Yes. Then there was Ben. She wasn't married to Ben, was she? They weren't engaged, were they? No. Did Ann want to be with him anyway? Yes. But Ann's parents couldn't be expected to appreciate any of this. They just expected her to come home for the summer as a matter of course. But they wouldn't stand in the way of her career. They would let her go to Aspen.

She could go for the second half of a six week program. She was shown to her room in the ski lodge where everybody had already been living for three weeks, where everybody already knew each other, where everybody was already in each other's rooms all the time. The guy with the crutch was already engaged to the girl who looked so morose, the girl with short hair was already in cosmic despair, and many cases of Cutty Sark had already been ordered from the liquor store. When Ann saw the man without shoes jump up and throw a bottle of Cutty Sark through the plate glass window she couldn't tell if this had happened before or not.

She sat on the edge of a chair in somebody's darkened room. Outside, the town was alternately dusty and muddy. Everybody seemed to be paired off—except for that boy with the blond hair, perhaps. His sulky expression might mean he was intelligent. They were high in a mountain valley surrounded by the Rocky Mountains deep in the interior of the continent. There was no escape. This was it. He was offering her some of his cheap wine so she could forget how they got up to her room and into her bed.

But after a few days she realized that she was just using him as a sexual object. She could let him rub Wesson oil on her, she could let him do almost anything to her, but what did he matter to her? He was a ski bum; he wasn't a writer. Since he was working construction for the summer she could try to feel romantic about his hard hat. Now she felt sufficiently jaded, enough to go downstairs and sit around with the others while they threw bottles of Cutty Sark through the windows.

The barefoot man took off all of his clothes so that Ann could paint designs on his body. Mrs. Zurmullen, Ann's third grade teacher, had told her mother that Ann would either be a great painter or a great writer or a great actress when she grew up if only she would stop sucking her thumb. Some things are foretold in prophecy. So they all danced Ann's paintings over to the condominium where the staff writer lived. He didn't let them in. The next day, Ann saw the staff writer skipping stone after stone on a lake. Was this the supreme act of futility? What reason did she have to go to Cheyenne, Wyoming for Frontier Days?

Ann's hard-hat said he was in love with her; he wanted to take her to Cheyenne, Wyoming for Frontier Days. Why not go, just like that, devil-may-care? It was way up on a back road where they had the flat. At least, Ann's life was in the hands of fate.

Ann walked out on the short dry grass under the porch. The girl with short hair who was in cosmic despair was standing there throwing rocks at a deflated car down in the ditch. Sometimes the rocks hit an old sink that was also down there. She was laughing. Ann put her hand in her pocket and felt the letter she had written to Ben. She walked inside past the translator who was saying "Did you have a good night, Ann?" She walked over to the mail slot. "Sure," she said. She wasn't about to tell him it had been great. Then she saw a remarkable person sitting next to the translator and sharing a map with him.

He was remarkable because he looked sane. The translator introduced them. He was Bob. It was as if they had known each other all their lives. He was sane, kind, and intelligent, just as she secretly was. Now that Bob was here she would throw off her disguise. He was obviously her port in a storm, he was her remembrance of things past, he was her link with real life. He was going to Marble with the translator. Ann rushed upstairs to get rid of her towel. She was going with them, wherever it was.

When she opened her door she found her hard-hat still lying in her bed with a little weird smile on his face. "Have you been swimming?" he asked. "No, whatever gave you that idea," she said, grabbing her camera and slamming the door.

In the car, Ann sat between Bob and the translator. Bob was wearing blue jeans and glasses. She talked with Bob about poetry. He loved the poets she loved, and hated the poets she hated. The translator probably wanted to be the one who got to sit in the middle.

They parked the car in front of the Marble Hotel. The translator went inside to inquire about the ancient prospector. As soon as he was out of the car, Ann and Bob started to talk about him. But he was back soon with a report: the ancient prospector had died last week, the jeep left for the quarry in forty minutes, and there was small lake to look at nearby.

Ann was watching Bob who had stopped on the trail ahead to light his pipe. She liked a man with a pipe—she liked, indeed, his smooth complexion, the dark hair curling at the nape of his neck, his clean white shirt, his blue jeans, his hips. His hips! His hips were too large. "Oh, my goodness!" said the translator, consulting his watch. "It's almost time."

It was night when they got to Cheyenne. The streets were full of beer bottles; cowboys and whores were dancing on the tables in the saloons. Everything smelled of liquor and sweat. Perhaps this was an ugly scene. Where were they going to sleep? They went back to the car. Where were they going to sleep? They were going to sleep in the car, pulled off to the side of the road. When Ann woke up she was drenched in sweat. The sun was blazing in through the back window.

Back in Aspen everything was going on the same as usual. A foreigner reprimanded Ann for never having heard of him before. Wasn't he a famous translator? Ann didn't know if he was a famous translator or not, she just knew he wanted to cook a duck for her and her hard-hat in her kitchenette. All right, let him. Then she would stop all this nonsense. She wasn't going to be here forever. Let him cook a fancy dinner for them. Let him ply them with wine. He kept talking about what a beautiful couple they were. It started to make Ann sick. Duck was a little too rich for her. And now he wanted to get into bed with the both of them. Wasn't it enough that Ann was using the hard-hat as a sexual object? This wasn't real life, but still. Everything seemed a bit too much. Ann had to give the translator a shove to get him out of the room. She locked the door after him. Her hard-hat looked up at her from the bed. Now she would have to figure out a way to get rid of him. She sat down and wrote a letter to Ben. He was the only thing she could remember from life.

The next day when she came back to her room from her morning workshop her hard-hat was still there. He was drinking wine and taking little morphine pills and smoking pot and flicking the ashes on the rug. There were beer cans by the bed, and one was overturned, so that there was a pool of beer on the rug. Ann was seeing her room, as it were, for the first time. There were big flies on the window ledge. Ann could squash them with her hand; they didn't try to fly away. He poured some 7-Up into a glass with some wine and handed it to her. She didn't take it. He was eating potato chips in bed. How was she going to get rid of him?

She would go swimming! That would show him. She would go swimming and not tell him she was going and she wouldn't ask him to come. That would really show him. When she got downstairs with her towel the pool was closed.

They all climbed into a jeep with a bunch of other people. The jeep began to move, and now it was time for Bob to use his movie camera. He took a lot of footage of the inside of Ann's mouth. He was a poet.

"Oh, crashing cascades fiercely falling," a girl said.

"Fierce isn't the half of it, dear," an older woman replied. "You see, dear," she said, "I think it was during World War II. Some soldiers got trapped in a very desolate place, just like this one. And, would you believe, it was the old ones who survived. The young ones didn't know how. Young people don't know how to survive. That's what they found out. So they started this survival school here. They send you out in the wilderness without anything to protect you. It's the truth. You can't come back till your time is up."

When they got back to the lodge, Bob let Ann use his credit card to make a phone call to Ben. Then Bob made a phone call to a great poet in New York, to give him Ann's astrological fix, so he could do her chart. Ann felt that at last steps were being taken to determine where she stood. She marched upstairs to confront her hard-hat.

He had been reading what she had written about him, and he was sulking. "Well, you shouldn't have looked at my stuff without my knowledge," she said. At last he must see her as she really was. Now he could hate her as much as she hated him. That was a load off her chest. Now her conscience was clear.

He was asking her to go to New York with him in the morning. He was going to New York, and she could be back in a week. The idea of going to New York was fun. On the road. Metropolis. No, really, it sounded great, but she had better not. He should go. He would have a marvelous time. She was sure to envy him. It was only for a week. "I'll pack you a lunch," she said, almost tenderly. Soon she was ready to go downstairs and hear some poetry.

The guest poet that night read a long poem about a house with a hundred rooms. In each room was a woman. They were all for him. Bob pointed out two women to Ann who were sitting in the front row. One was the poet's wife, and the other was his mistress. They had all three arrived in Aspen that morning. Ann wondered how the women felt to be in competition with ninety-eight others. It was time to go to bed.

Her hard-hat was asleep when she came into the room. She could see him in the half-light from the bathroom. All the muscles in his face were relaxed. The sheet had fallen back from the smooth chest of Adonis. He was a beautiful blond one. But she was no Tonio Kroeger. She didn't wake until he had left.

At last she was alone in her room. She rushed out to her morning workshop. She returned to her room. She had her room all to herself. She went over to where Bob was staying to see if he wanted to go swimming.

She had to consider first whether she wanted Bob to see her body. Well, it was all right if it was in the context of swimming. It couldn't be construed as anything else. You had to get undressed to go swimming. What she liked about Bob was that she could talk with him.

Bob did not want to go swimming. Ann wondered if Bob said he didn't want to go swimming just because he didn't want to go swimming. She wondered if he didn't want to show his body to her or if he just wanted to keep her in his bedroom with him.

He told her he was really into his body. He practiced Tai Chi. It was a discipline of enormous grace. Ann felt absolutely at home as she watched Bob doing Tai Chi positions on the rug. There was a discreet knock at the door. Bob's position changed to door opening.

Ann watched Bob talking softly to someone on the other side of the door. Then she saw him take a tea tray from the girl of cosmic despair. "That was Luna," Bob said, turning towards Ann with the tea tray. On the tray was a teapot and two cups. One for Bob and one for Luna.

Ann looked over at the little doorway which led into the alcove. She pictured herself hanging upside down in the door by one foot, she told Bob. "Just like the Hanged Man in the Tarot Deck," Bob said. But Ann had never seen a Tarot Deck, so Bob explained that she was in a state of suspension. How understanding he was. There was Adonis, whom she had just managed to get rid of, and Ben, whom she was separated from. "Of course, in certain cases, the card connotes selfishness," Bob went on. Bob was leaving for San Francisco tomorrow. Ann was desolate. When he was gone, Ann would have no one to talk to.

She wished she could go to San Francisco too. Why couldn't she go? Because the writing program wouldn't be over yet. Well, why couldn't she miss the end? She could go and spend a few days in

Berkeley with Ben before she was expected back in Beverly Hills. And, what's more, she could vanish before Adonis returned!

Ann had a lot of packing to do. Her room was a mess. She put on a record and started with Ben's letters. She sat down on the floor and started to read them all over again. There was no one to look over her shoulder. There was a knocking.

It was Luna, the girl of cosmic despair. The girl who threw rocks. She was holding a Billie Holiday record in one hand and a Pyrex measuring cup in the other. The measuring cup held the remains of some Cutty Sark. She smiled. "Is that Bach you're reading?" she asked, coming in and pouring herself some wine. "If I went to Detroit, I'd work for G.M.," she said, leveling with Ann.

"No, don't go to Detroit," Ann said, "have some more wine. Here's the last clean glass. I'm going to wash all the dishes. I'm going to find the vacuum, and I'm going to vacuum the rug. I'm going to empty all the ashtrays, and I'm going to drag a wet towel over the kitchen floor. Don't you think that's a good idea?"

"We should do some climbing," Luna said. "We should climb a mountain while we're here, because you can't do that in Detroit, at G.M."

"You're right," Ann said. "But I'm leaving for San Francisco tomorrow. I don't really want to stay for the end."

"No, I wouldn't really work there," Luna said. "The pay is terrific, but I couldn't really do it," Luna said. "It's not really Bach." She went over and put Billie Holiday on. Then she sat down on the rug, and taking a piece of paper from the table and a pen from the floor she drew a picture of the mouth of the soul.

Ann was ready when Bob pulled the rented station wagon up in front of the lodge, ready to load. She wasn't leaving anything behind. At the last minute, she had decided to take the record player Adonis had left behind. It was Adonis' record player, but she could take it as a present to Ben. Perhaps when Adonis returned he would at last understand. Bob helped her pack it in. There were three other people leaving the sinking ship with them. They would take turns, and drive straight through.

Just as they were pulling out, someone came running up to the car. It was Luna. Ann rolled down her window. "I just wanted to tell you not to come back!" Luna yelled. "I won't," Ann called, but Luna already had her back to them. The translator was taking their picture. Ann watched him and his camera and Luna and Aspen grow smaller.

"Isn't that the Bay over there?" someone in the car asked. Ann could feel her heart beating. Bob helped her carry her suitcase, typewriter, and record player into Ben's place. Ben showed Bob what corner to put everything down in. Any corner. They didn't want to keep Bob waiting. Ben and Bob shook hands. Suddenly, Bob was gone.

Ben smelled like Ben! There was his beard and his face. There were his pipe and his slippers. There was the desk where he worked. Ann was sitting on Ben's lap.

"I've been on the road," she told him.

"That's cool," he said.

"I've been through miles of boring countryside without sleeping," she said.

"Right," Ben said.

"I've been through the Donner Pass where people eat each other," Ann went on, shifting in Ben's lap. "I had a Chinese dinner in Utah."

"It doesn't matter, you're here now," he said. They started to kiss.

"Look! I brought you a record player!" she said. "Now we can have music!"

"That's fantastic," he said. "A fantastic coincidence. A friend of mine was through here last week and left me a record player. We can give the one you brought to Beth." Beth was the wife Ben used to live with.

"That's a good idea," Ann said. "She needs it."

Ben put on a record. They got into bed. It was eleven o'clock in the morning. Just about now, an old man in a top hat was getting the Nobel Prize. Nothing else in the world had really ever happened.

The Map of Happy Valley

THIS WAS NO ORDINARY AIRPLANE. It was a bit shakier than other airplanes, but it was perfectly safe, and the fare was cheap. It was some sort of business deal Father had done with this company. He laughingly called it Fly By Night Airways. Everyone was happy that Ann could be flown from Berkeley to L.A. so ingeniously. All of Ann's holiday visits home were thus taken care of for her. All she needed to do to transfer herself safely back to Beverly Hills was to think certain thoughts out of her head.

First was the memory of all the drugs she had ever taken. Second was the memory of all the political demonstrations and activities she had engaged in. Third was all the men she had ever slept with and the loss of her virginity itself. And fourth was the married man she was in love with. There. Now she wouldn't have to lie to her parents. With a huge backwards roar the plane came to ground.

There was her family on the end of the gangplank held in check by a velvet rope. She embraced each one while the others stood patiently by. Then a stranger stepped forward and took her in his arms. Everyone beamed approval.

This was no ordinary occasion. This was Chuck, from Portland, Oregon, the man who had proposed to Barbara. Barbara was engaged to be married; the slate was wiped clean.

All during Thanksgiving there was a constant round of activity during which the young lovers were hosted and toasted. Barbara was surprisingly beautiful fastening her pearls in front of the mirror in preparation for joining the grandmothers and aunts at the top of an elegant department store in the middle of a fashion show over lunch while Father and Chuck pushed a more important golf ball over the turf. Barbara bestowed a smile on Ann, and in that smile was forgiveness at last for that terrible thing Ann had done to Barbara when they were so small that their spindly legs dangled from the piano stool.

Neither of them had liked practising, but they were both in love with Mr. Schubert, who came to their living room every Thursday. This was a milestone in Ann and Barbara's lives because their parents had done some remodeling, and they were given a private bathroom of their very own. The mirrored dressing table was the most beautiful thing Ann had ever looked into. The doorbell rang, and Ann went to answer it. It was Mr. Schubert, a little bit early. "Oh, Mr. Schubert, there's something I'd like to show you!" Ann opened the door to the bathroom for Mr. Schubert. There was a scream. Then over Mr. Schubert's shoulder Ann saw Barbara sitting on the toilet tinkling away. That had been the end of their duets. What did *this* matter now when Barbara was in love and her love was returned?

For a moment Ann thought about telling Barbara about Ben. But then the joke in the family would be that she would be next. They would all ask her all about him. They would hear with horror that he was married; they wouldn't see the important point was that he was separated. They would cringe at the idea that he had a child—and by another woman, yet! They would think Ben's lovely beard was a nest for mice. She couldn't even tell them she was dating a professor, because Ben wasn't actually a professor. He was an acting instructor, a graduate student. There was no name for what she and Ben had between them. Ann never knew from week to week when she would see him. She did not want to name it for fear it would go away. There was nothing she could say.

So she told them about this place to walk she had discovered in Berkeley. It was a part of Berkeley you would never know was there. It was Happy Valley. "Happy Valley?" her family asked. "Well, I call it Happy Valley," Ann said. Then she proceeded to describe to them the architecture and foliage of the walk between her place and Ben's apartment, naming all the secret staircases between the winding roads, but not Ben's apartment, and the overhanging branches, the crooked sidewalks, the two strong pillars you must walk through, the blossoming tree in the moonlight. "In the moonlight?" her family asked.

For a moment, Ann was at a loss for words. Then Grandma said, "You better sew that button on tighter or you're going to lose it."

The Heart in the Bahamas

ANN LOVED TO SIT with her bay windows open at twilight and the purple wind off the Bay pulsing through. Soon all this would end. In a few days, when she was called back to Beverly Hills for the summer. Ordinarily, she would have been flown south already, as soon as the semester was over. School had already been out for a week. But she was existing in a state of grace. Her parents had gone to the Bahamas. That in itself was exciting, but they would all be back in Beverly Hills soon enough. Ann was looking down, looking to see Ben come winding down the paths from Happy Valley. Half of the time Ann went there but half of the time Ben came here. Then a dark car pulled up. It was Ben getting out the passenger side. A stranger got out the other. They both came inside.

Ben winked at Ann. The stranger took off his hat, but not his dark glasses. He sat by the window with his hands folded over his black sweater. He was Popov. What did that mean to Ann? An artifact from Ben's former life. The story of the party when Popov had gone to the bathroom, how he failed to reappear, how they had broken in the door to find the bathroom was empty and Popov was gone. And how, ever after that, cutting out without warning was "doing a popov." Popov had appeared suddenly out of nowhere, so Ben had brought him here.

Ann did her best to amuse him, taking out her curiosities one by one—here is a stuffed baby alligator in a hula skirt her sister had sent from her honeymoon in Jamaica. Here is a scooped-out armadillo with emerald green rhinestones in its eyesockets—a purse Ann had picked up in Mexico. Here is a house which is really a mushroom which is really a bank. Here is a black bat, with a face like a rat, hanging from the curtain. Popov stood up and picked up his hat. "I suppose this is one of your little pets?" he asked. Ann and Ben were leaping out of their chairs. It was a *bat*, hanging upside down.

"Is it gone?" Ann called from the other room.

"Yes, it's safe," Ben said, opening the door. Popov was closing the window. "Popov shook the curtain," Ben said.

Ann was very grateful to Popov. And grateful when he left. She and Ben had so little time left together. Soon they would be torn asunder. Ben took Ann in his arms. Soon they were asleep.

They woke up in the middle of the night. They had neglected to turn out the light. Ben went down the hall to the bathroom, Ann switched off the light and crawled under the covers. This high pitched sound wasn't normal. This high pitched sound was not normal. It was flying round and round the room—a horrible bat! Ann was screaming. An eternity passed. Then Ben rushed in and switched on the light. So the thing hung on the curtain again, upside down. They sat on the bed and looked at it. Now they would have to deal with it. It wasn't easily got rid of.

The next night at twilight they stood in the street looking up at Ann's window. Ann had called the inspector. He found no guano. There were no bats. But if they wanted to, they could stand out in the street at twilight and watch for bats to come. It was becoming clear to them that there was no point in watching for what might never appear. It was getting hard to see. Perhaps they could forget it really happened. So they went back inside, to hold each other tight against the night. The phone was ringing.

"Hello, Ann? This is a friend of your parents."

Ann hastened to tell him that her folks would be back in Beverly Hills in a few days, but right now they were in the—

"The Bahamas is where I'm calling from," he said. "Your father's going to be all right. He's had a heart attack."

There was a silence in which Ann fished around for a face. Her suitcase was already packed. That was convenient. A shameful convenience. The weather was clear. That was inappropriate. This was an airplane. Ann was leaving Ben on the ground.

This was a person in sunglasses flying through the empty night to the Bahamas, the glamorous Bahamas. It was a sin to see any glamor in flying there.

Ann looked out the window trying to think of what had not been done that might never be. An image of a black-shrouded widow and orphan kneeling by the graveside in the gray rain was playing. It was cheap. This was not a romance.

It happened to everybody. That was a fact. It happened to other people, and other people's people. That was the sense of it. Was Ann being called upon to confront the universe?

She was trying to think of the right promise to make and the right person to make it to to get out of it. But that was sentimental, and she couldn't. This was a taxi cab.

This was simply a hospital. This was the end of it. Ann's father was recovering.

That was all there was to it. Ann's father was weak, but in three weeks he would be strong. They would be three weeks in the Bahamas.

Ann and her mother shared a motel room close to the hospital. They were all so happy that Ann was there. They spoke of why this had happened. The ice cream, the act of God. Why didn't he take more vacations? Why had he taken this one? Why was he stricken? Why was he spared? Because they cared? Why should he continue to recover? Because Ann was there? She changed the subject. She was thinking of Ben.

Ann visited her father in the hospital every day. They played gin rummy the same as usual. Ann's father spoke of how he was going to live his life better. He was going to cut down on the pressure. The work was piling up every minute he was away.

One day, shortly before they returned to Beverly Hills, Ann stood on a beach just the way a person does who is on vacation. She wanted to run back to the hospital to make sure her father was still alive. She wanted to tell him how much she loved him. She wished she could promise always to be his little girl. She stepped into the clear salt water. It soothed the bites from the mosquitoes which the sea breezes had failed to blow away. Somebody told her this was the most beautiful beach in the world. She knew it was a very beautiful place when she asked herself if she would like to be here with Ben. But it was wasted on her. She was so far away.

Right now all of her prayers were due to her father. But she was thinking of Ben. A wave of nausea washed over her. She couldn't tell her father about Ben. How she was hoping to move in with Ben when she returned to Berkeley in the fall. How she was tormented with the possibility that Ben would change his mind towards her in the meantime. That he would do a popov. That he would forget she ever existed. Her father was innocent of all knowledge of Ben. Her father had nearly lost his life. And she was planning to deceive him.

She shaded her eyes with her hand and scanned the horizon. She must look to her mother like she was innocently engaged. She was afraid that her face was the same as her mind. She must not be a source of worry to her mother. Her mother was relying on her. Ann couldn't let her down.

And she couldn't live without Ben. She phrased a letter to him in her mind. "The water is dark purple," she tried. But that wasn't it. The water was blue.

She reached down in the shallow water and picked up a sponge. "A millionaire's plaything," she wrote in her head. Then she examined it. It looked like an ordinary sponge which anybody could buy in a store. But it was rather larger, with two chambers. It looked like a human heart. It was disgusting.

Hawaiian Bargain

ANN AND BEN found an unfurnished apartment on the north side of Berkeley and furnished it with tables and chairs cast off from friends and a big green couch which they had gotten really cheap at St. Vincent de Paul. The furniture was, however, barely noticeable under the stacks of books and papers with which graduate students feather their nests. Ann was in constant anxiety that the landlady, Mrs. Teapot, would come in before she had had a chance to clear away the books and papers or wash the wall over the fireplace, which was quite black because they had such lovely fires in the fireplace.

So from time to time Ann went to visit Mrs. Teapot, to make a social call the way any respectable married woman would and talk about what any respectable married woman always had on her mind—her husband's pants, how he wanted them pressed, what he liked to eat, how hard he worked. How hard he worked! And late into the night. He should never be disturbed. Mrs. Teapot must never barge in on them to see what Ann only saw when she looked at it through Mrs. Teapot's eyes—the incredible chaos of Ann's housekeeping.

There was not only incredible chaos, there was real dirt. Ann should feel ashamed of herself. Ann felt ashamed of herself when she thought of Mrs. Teapot coming. She would ask Mrs. Teapot what kind of wax was best to use on a hardwood floor. Ann hadn't waxed the floor yet. She was waiting for the best wax. Ann had wished that the floors would have come to her attention sooner. But she had not noticed them with all the clothes and books and papers and shoes and cups on them.

Actually, Ann didn't know what to make of Mrs. Teapot, Mrs. Teapot who had loaned them some of her own furniture which they had to take care of. Ann should feel grateful to Mrs. Teapot for renting this apartment to them as a pair of romantic newlyweds. If only she wouldn't ask why Ann's mail continued to come addressed to her maiden name.

Or why Ann left at Thanksgiving, Christmas, and Easter vacations, and Ben stayed in the apartment. Although that would have been easily explained by the fact that Ann's father was quite sick, and Ann had to fly down to L.A. to be with him whenever a school holiday afforded an opportunity, while the pressure of Ben's studies kept him in Berkeley. But most probably Mrs. Teapot had never deserted Mr. Teapot on a holiday.

And Ann's father, actually, was not exactly sick, although it was true that he had had a heart attack once in the Bahamas. It was just that her parents expected that she would come home for the holidays as a matter of course. She didn't have any excuse not to. She couldn't say that she would rather stay in her apartment with her roommate Nancy. That would sound even worse than actually telling them she was living with Ben and didn't want to leave him for a day.

If Ann's parents had known, or had admitted that they knew that Ann wasn't really living with Nancy, but was actually living with Ben, a man, they might have understood why she wanted to stay in Berkeley. But it would have been nothing compared with their utter horror, shame, disgust, and whatnot. Ann might have told her parents that she was living with Ben even so, if it had not been for the fact that Ann's father had had a heart attack once in the Bahamas.

This Easter vacation, however, she wouldn't be going to L.A. Her parents were taking her to Hawaii. Father's business was mill, which was small, but made to scale, over to the lily-pad pool without crossing the driveway. Carol Kaufman always made a big deal about crossing the driveway. Why would a car come up just at the moment when they were crossing? Ann was under Carol Kaufman's spell, and she ran after Carol Kaufman crossing the driveway as if there really was danger. Then suddenly a huge black shiny car was there. A small shrunken mean bent man was getting out of his car shaking a stick at them and screaming at them to get off his estate! Get off his estate!

Ann had thought that the most important thing about Faust was that he had made a bargain with the devil. When she thought about it, she wondered if it wasn't the nature of the bargain Faust had made that was so important. It was, on the surface, a fairly easy bargain—in Faust's favor. All Faust had to remember to do was to never say to the passing moment "Abide, thou art so fair." Ann wondered if she would be able to remember not to say it if she were in the same situation.

But, as it turned out, neither was the important thing about Faust. The important thing about Faust, Ann learned from the lecturer that night, was that he had a will to power. As a supreme example of Faustian man, men who had a supreme will to power, the lecturer gave the example of certain people who had left many many years ago from what is now North Viet Nam in small boats with which they somehow managed to navigate themselves to the Polynesian Islands which had previously been undiscovered and uninhabited. What a will to power they must have had to embark on such a daring venture. When they got there the climate was extremely healthy, the sky usually cloudless or only partly cloudy. They could pluck all the fruit they wanted and there weren't any poisonous snakes.

The Hawaii these people found, the lecturer pointed out, was Eden. At no other time or place in history, either before or since, have people been so completely freed from the worry and business of food and shelter. This was the golden age which other people had always waited for the coming of while they went about trammeled in their daily lives, laying one brick on another.

The Hawaiians were especially licentious upon the death of a king, and between times they were busy with human sacrifices whenever a temple was to be dedicated, or a chief was sick, or a war booming; everything he touched turned to gold. That night, Ann and Ben attended a lecture on campus entitled "Faustian Man and the Coming of the Golden Age."

Ann had an idea who Faust was. She knew of him mainly through looking at a photo of Harold Lloyd which they had on their wall. Harold Lloyd looked ridiculous. He was hanging onto the enormous hands of some clock high on a building. And the clock was about to strike. Underneath the photo Ben had inscribed "O lente, lente, currite noctis equii!" He said it meant "Run slowly, slowly, horses of the night." It was from Marlowe's *Faustus*. This was especially appropriate because sometime before they had stapled a large billboard picture of horses running to the wall above where the photo of Harold Lloyd later got stapled. Sometimes Ann worried that Mrs. Teapot would barge in and see the staples in her wall. Harold Lloyd had thought he looked ridiculous hanging onto the hands of a clock, looking down on what he was about to strike. But actually it was the quote from *Faustus* under him which made him look really ridiculous, Ann thought.

Ann had met Harold Lloyd once. This was one of the little details of Ann's life which Ben found particularly charming, in that Ann had not only met Harold Lloyd but found him to be a person to be despised. Actually, Ann had not so much *met* Harold Lloyd as met up with him. Ann had had no desire to meet Harold Lloyd. She didn't even know who he was.

When Ann and Carol Kaufman crawled through the drainpipe onto the Harold Lloyd Estate they were not going there to see Harold Lloyd, or be part of *his* world, whatever that was. They were going to see the Harold Lloyd Estate, and be part of that world. That was a world of a real leafy forest that you could almost not see the boundaries of once you were in it, real baby waterfalls, and an actual facsimile of a mill, right in the middle of Beverly Hills. The Harold Lloyd Estate was more than one world. On the other side of the driveway was another world, with a long rectangular swimming pool in solitude. In the pool floated real lily pads, and stately columns stood all around. The columns had once been white, but were now the color of timelessness, where nobody goes. Nobody but Ann and Carol Kaufman.

The most dangerous part of the estate, and the only part which wasn't real, was the driveway. There was no way to get from the was to be undertaken, and these occasions were frequent.

It is remarkable to think that with all the time they had on their hands they produced no culture at all. No written language. No systems of knowledge. They produced a little tapa cloth, and that about wraps it up.

Then the lecturer painted a picture of another golden age which was just now coming, the golden age of the perfection of technology which had just about learned to reproduce nature at its most bountiful in the shapes of high-rise apartments where all the trammels of daily life had been seen to, and where there was a recreation room and sauna in the basement. Faustian man had had the will to power to crack the DNA code, and now all there was left to do was sort out the details.

This was the first in a series of lectures the lecturer was giving. In the rest of the lectures, the lecturer was going to lecture on the endless predictable information which was all there was left to sort out since the cracking of the DNA code, which was the last discovery there was to be. Ann and Ben didn't attend the rest of the lectures.

Ann had caught a cold—just a few days before she was supposed to leave for Hawaii. Not that a cold could keep her from leaving. Pneumonia might have kept her at home, but Ann would never have gone that far. That would be sick. The cold was just a little physical manifestation of her vexation, or else it was her guilt flowing over, guilt for not being the noble girl who doesn't mind leaving her true love for a mere week, her true love whom she wouldn't be living with under such circumstances. Or else it was guilt for not forsaking everything—all propriety—for her love which burns like a single steady flame.

It wasn't really what one wanted when one was going to Hawaii, the place where the trade winds blow, where one can swim further and further out to the coral reef, the place where romance was always in flower.

Ann blew her nose. She and Ben had resolved to send each other messages by ESP while she was away in order somehow to keep in touch. They knew it was only an expedient measure. What could they transmit over thousands of miles of emptiness?

As Ann's plane gained altitude and swung out over the ocean towards Hawaii, Ben, back in the apartment fixing his own lunch, was transmitting thoughts like "Oh, why did you put the peanut butter in a place where I can't find it?"

Just then Ann was trying to pop her ears. The plane had landed in Honolulu. No one was there to greet them at the airport. No one gave Ann a lei. Her ears didn't pop.

After they had checked into their hotel—the Outrigger Hotel on Waikiki Beach—they took a stroll to the office of an ear doctor, and checked into Ann's head. She was locked inside there. So they gave her a shot in the arm, some bitter pills to take, and the precaution to keep her head above water.

She wore a scarf when they rode in the catamaran. She sent messages to Ben: blue, blue-green; blue, blue-green. Out here far from the shore there were flying fish. At least other people in the boat said that they were spotting them. The water gleamed blue, bright and deep, and the swell began to surge back towards the high-rise hotels and apartments which were the shore.

On this vacation they were not going to break their necks being tourists. They had seen all the scenery that everybody else was rushing around to look at before. They were just going to lie around on the beach and enjoy themselves. Ann lay on the beach with her parents, reading. Soon she would be able to send Ben the message that she had already finished one half of *This Side of Paradise.*

And she thought how this was Monday, and then there was Tuesday, and after that Wednesday left only two days to the day before the date she would be home. But she was getting used to it now, walking down the street in the warm air in her sun dress with her parents to Woody's Cafeteria with all the others—the newly-weds and the nearly-deads, who were also walking in their sun dresses and other new clothes to Woody's Cafeteria.

Ann and her family passed through, and walked on, onto the grounds of the Royal Hawaiian Hotel. They walked through its gardens, and went down its corridors, and past its arcades, and into its lobby, where a few old women were talking. The Royal Hawaiian Hotel still had a lot of elegance, but not that much, and it seemed almost dead. It made Ann sort of sad.

Because Carol Kaufman, the Carol Kaufman who had stayed at the Royal Hawaiian when it was the *only* place to stay, the Carol Kaufman who had disclosed to her the mystery of the Harold Lloyd

Estate, the Carol Kaufman of limber grace, a flash of blond hair in the sunlight while she alternately tanned and swam in the pool, because Carol Kaufman of the charmingly turned-up nose had grown into a distorted thing like Alice, on two huge legs with dishwater hair and a nose that was still growing. Because Carol Kaufman had worn big ugly dresses and went steady with a dolt, a person who embodied none of the mystery of which the Harold Lloyd Estate was an example. Because Carol Kaufman was no more to Ann, and had been no one to her for years. But now she was here, linked to this big pink hotel.

Ann's father rented a car, and drove them to that part of the island which they had not previously been to, Koko Head. They had not previously been there because the last time they were in Hawaii Koko Head had, for all intents and purposes, not previously been there. Because the Kahala Hilton had not been built then. In the past, there had not even been the possibility of staying at the Kahala Hilton.

They visited the Kahala Hilton as outsiders. Walking into the dining room at the Kahala Hilton they almost didn't notice the sunken pools which appeared on either side of the path. In the sunken pools swam porpoises, tortoises, and blowfish. It was incredible, but it was just part of the decor. If it became more than part of the decor to you you were not sufficiently important. Because then the Kahala Hilton was more important than you. The Kahala Hilton had absorbed the function of the old Royal Hawaiian; that is where that function had gone.

Ann and her family went on, back to revisit the Hawaiian Village, and found that it had become incredibly crass and commercial, not to mention plastic and sleazy. They were glad that they were staying at the Outrigger this time. The Outrigger was neutral, and didn't have to do with either the past or the future. Which wasn't to say it had much to do with the present, for Ann, at least. The present was going on in Berkeley without her. Ann was on her way to lunch at a tea-room on Oahu.

This time they didn't visit the Robert Louis Stevenson shack. They were aware it was out back, just the same as it was nine years ago. There was still all the fruit cocktail they could eat.

Ann noticed that her mother had started to cry into her fruit cocktail. She was crying because everything was the same, but

Barbara wasn't there. Barbara wasn't with them like she was nine years ago because she was happily married and living in Portland, Oregon. Ann felt obligated to say a few words of regret that Barbara wasn't with them, but she didn't want to. She didn't wish that Barbara was there, she wished that Ben was there. She had wished that Ben was there for the whole vacation. But *she* couldn't cry into *her* fruit cocktail. She didn't want to hurt her parents' feelings.

It was irrational of Mother to feel sad that Barbara wasn't there. She should feel happy that Barbara was happy. Feeling sad was a waste of a happy vacation. After all, Ann reasoned with her, it wasn't that often that she and Daddy got to be with her, Ann, anymore. They should take advantage of this opportunity of the three of them being together with no cares or worries in a wonderful place.

They decided to cheer up and go to a movie. Ann was really glad to be going to a movie. For one thing, she and Ben never went to first-run movies in Berkeley because they disdained them. There weren't any good first-run movies in America anymore, even if Ann and Ben could afford to go to them. Besides, Ann was glad that they were going to a movie because she knew that while they were at the movies she would be safe from any questions her parents might naturally ask about her life in Berkeley and her roommate Nancy. She had been in terror that her parents would ask her about her roommate Nancy for the entire trip. Her parents had never asked anything about her roommate Nancy. Apparently they didn't care what kind of a person the only daughter they had left to them was living with. From time to time Ann had tried to bring Nancy up in the conversation. "Nancy's such a slob," she had said to her mother on the beach. "I'm afraid to go home and see what a mess she has made of the apartment." "You'd better put some suntan lotion on," her mother had said. "I think you're getting a burn." And later Ann had said casually, "I hope Nancy's feeding our cat. I hope Nancy remembers to feed the cat while I'm away. Nancy never thinks about feeding the cat. I always have to feed the cat." And Mother had said, "What does your cat eat? Our cat won't eat anything but liver." Apparently, Mother was more interested in talking about cats than she was in talking about Ann's roommate, Nancy. Apparently, she had no interest in Ann's roommate

Nancy at all. Nancy was a person, and a very big part of their daughter's world, and they weren't interested in her. "No, they're not really interested in the real me," Ann thought.

She leaned back in her loge seat between her parents. Only a few years ago, she thought, she would have felt embarrassed going to a movie with her parents. Not because of her parents themselves, but because they were proof she wasn't on a date. Proof, to all these ugly strangers. She was glad she wasn't like that anymore.

The movies they were about to see were "The Graduate," which was about what life was really like when you grew up in Beverly Hills and went to school at Berkeley, and "The Fox," which was based on a D. H. Lawrence story about lesbians. Mother and Ann had been careful not to tell Father what these movies were about beforehand. They had been lucky to get him to take them to these movies, even so, because he knew they weren't war or cowboy movies. Father usually didn't see any point in going to movies what were going to bore you, that weren't good family entertainment.

"The Graduate" came on. It started in Beverly Hills, a few blocks from where Ann's parents lived. There was supposed to be a sense of alienation in the swimming pool, which could have been Ann's parents' swimming pool, where Dustin Hoffman, who was supposed to represent Ann, was wearing the diving gear which had been strapped on as a graduation present. The woman who was carrying a tray of clinking glasses out to the glass table by the pool with her hair done was an actress who was supposed to be Dustin Hoffman's mother, who was supposed to be Ann's mother. All the little details were very accurate, but Ann resented being represented by Dustin Hoffman. Actually, Dustin Hoffman was the kind of person Ann had been running from for her whole life. Now Mrs. Robinson was seducing Dustin Hoffman. Mrs. Robinson was also supposed to represent Ann's mother. Mr. Robinson had a huge color t.v. set. Ann's father was turning white.

Now Dustin Hoffman and Mrs. Robinson's daughter, who was a beautiful girl who never had to worry if her hair got wet and represented a person Ann was supposed to hope she was represented by, were going out on a date together. Now the awful truth was out and Dustin Hoffman was looking for her at U.S.C., which was represented as Berkeley. But really all of the real Berkeley you could see was what could be seen from a bus. Berkeley was a place Dustin Hoffman could get to only by driving the wrong way on the Oakland Bay Bridge. He did not even notice that everyone else was going the wrong way.

But when the lights came on everything was gone. Mother, played by Mrs. Robinson, was laughing, and Father, who was white, said that he was going out for a coke.

The next movie, "The Fox," was sad. Not because a beautiful lesbian relationship was broken up by a man, but because the people in the movie had to wear not only sweaters, but jackets, and big quilts, because it was cold. It was cold the way it never is in Beverly Hills. The way it never is in Hawaii. And it was, actually, a lot colder than it was in Berkeley. But at least you had to wear a jacket in Berkeley. And so Ann was reminded of Berkeley again, although she didn't want to be. It was too painful. Too far away. But it wasn't the end of the world, just the end of the evening as the technicolor faded and the lights came on again. They woke Father up and walked back to the hotel.

It was the next morning. Ann was on the plane back to Berkeley. Ann was climbing the steps. She was carrying her suitcase, but Mrs. Teapot was nowhere in sight. She was inside.

"I meant to have the place picked up before you got here," Ben said. "Mrs. Teapot was over while you were gone. The old cat's been very restless. I think he missed you. The nights were very long. Did you send messages? I forgot to. Hey, you know what? We're out of cat food. You don't have to take another vacation for a while, do you? Nancy was over and brought us some grass. It was grown in Hawaii. I have a joint here all rolled up."

The shades were pulled down over the bedroom windows, closing out Mrs. Teapot's apartment. And the curtain was pulled across. The quilts were pulled back from the sheet. Ann and Ben lay naked in the bed, smoking. Ann and Ben lay in the bed stroking. The morning light shone around the edges of the curtain.

So Ann might well have said to the passing moment, "Abide, thou art so fair." Rightfully, she belonged to the devil, but the angels came up from underneath and carried her away.

ing, if you can imagine. These are the last few days I'll have my little girl! Did you take a look at our scores from this morning yet? I'm surprised we did so well!"

"Constantinople?" Mrs. Ladyfriend inquired politely. "I thought Constantinople was in Asia."

"I think it's got to be one of these places you can only get to once every hundred years," Father chuckled. "I couldn't find it on the map! Are you sure this place exists?" he asked Ann. "Listen men," he said, suddenly serious, turning to address Mother and Ann. "I've got to run to that meeting now. Meet you back here between five-thirty and six."

"The man Ann is going to marry got a job somewhere in the middle of nowhere!" Mother said to Mrs. Ladyfriend.

"Where will I find you? Here or in the room?" Father said.

"It's in the country," Ann said.

"Here, or in the room?" Father asked.

"Still, we should probably have bid one no-trump in that last hand," Mother said to Mrs. Ladyfriend.

"Here, or in the room?" Father said to Mother.

"In the Grand Ballroom," Mother said, turning to him. "The afternoon session will still be going on," she was saying when Father bent down and gave Ann a kiss. His business suit was very well tailored and really quite handsome. Then he and his briefcase melted from the lobby. Mother and Mrs. Ladyfriend had turned and were walking towards the judges' tables outside the Grand Ballroom. Silver and linen were everywhere. Marble pillars, gilt ceilings!

"And how do you think you'll like living in the country?" Mrs. Ladyfriend inquired politely when Mother exchanged a few words with another person neither Ann nor Mrs. Ladyfriend knew.

"I know I'm going to love it," Ann said.

Ann just wasn't being polite. The fact was, she already did love it. Because she was already living in the country. For although Ann had told her parents all summer that she was living in Berkeley with a woman, in actuality she had moved up to Bloomfield with Ben as soon as school was out in the spring. There they were, making a vegetable garden in what once was a goat pen under the eucalyptus beside the dark cypress! From there they could see forever and ever and only the sun and the moon could see them.

A Wedding in the Country

AND WHERE ARE YOU and your husband going to be living after the honeymoon?" Mrs. Ladyfriend, Mother's bridge partner, was asking Ann. They were all standing in the lobby of what had once been one of San Francisco's finest hotels. Light shone down through clear windows into the interior court and onto the potted palms.

"Constantinople," Ann answered Mrs. Ladyfriend. They had all agreed that they were lucky to be staying here. It had a lot more charm than some of the newer hotels. Besides, the bridge tournament where Mother and Mrs. Ladyfriend were playing was taking place here. Mother and Mrs. Ladyfriend were lucky to run into each other here. "Actually," Mother confided to Mrs. Ladyfriend, "I wouldn't have come up for this this year if it weren't for the fact that Ann is getting married."

"It's a small town about sixty miles north of here," Ann explained to Mrs. Ladyfriend. "Actually, we'll be living on the *outskirts* of Constantinople," Ann said. "On top of a hill above a place called Bloomfield."

"That's where Ann's wedding's going to be," Mother explained to Mrs. Ladyfriend. "We're all going up for it on Saturday morn-

They walked naked in the garden and swam in a pond that was the eye of the sky; they were in paradise! Except for the lie Ann had to tell to her parents about where she was living since they would have found it somehow shameful that she was living with Ben before she had married him—either wrong or stupid. But soon—starting on Saturday—she would be freed of this lying forever! She and Ben would be married!

After they were married Ann would no longer dread the day when her parents discovered that she was living with Ben. She would not be obliged to leave Ben for holidays or for ever!

Ann stood in the hallway looking through the two huge doors in the style of Louis Quatorze into the Grand Ballroom—delicate off-white, gold leaf, card tables, grand and refined space of high ceiling gradually filling up with cigarette smoke. Yes, everything was wonderful, wonderful! But there was a hitch. Ben was still married to Bobby's mother, Beth.

For although Benjamin and Elizabeth had been separated for years they had not gotten around to getting an official divorce—a frightening and costly proceding. But now it was unavoidable. Ann couldn't live in the country forever telling her parents that she was in Berkeley! She couldn't go on lying to landlords and employers over a piece of paper. Ben would have to get a divorce—and before his new job started in the fall. There would, in fact, be just time for it to go through.

Just time. They had thought there would be more time. They had miscalculated somehow. The divorce would not be through until the very day before the day they had already set for the wedding. The invitations had already gone out.

Then Mother had discovered the bridge tournament. And Father had discovered a convention he could profitably attend at the same time in Frisco. So they had rented a hotel room and had a cot brought into it for almost nothing so that Ann could spend her last virgin moments in the bosom of her parents. Ann was relieved that the divorce was coming due the day before the day set for the wedding and not the day after. She didn't want to have to change the date. She didn't want to have to get involved in telling her parents any more lies. She had told her parents years ago that Ben was already divorced. Fortunately, it could all work out without anybody being the wiser.

Still, it was going to be complicated. For since the divorce was not going to come due until the day before the wedding Ann and Ben couldn't buy a license until the day before the wedding. And since they were scheduled to be married in Sonoma County, they would have to buy the marriage license in Sonoma County. Somehow, the divorce, which, it turned out, was a piece of paper like a diploma, would have to be gotten from the courthouse in Oakland and transported the sixty miles to the courthouse in Santa Rosa on Friday, not Saturday when courthouses are closed. That meant Ann was going to have to leave her parents' bosom for several hours on Friday without them thinking that it was somehow weird.

So the next morning, in the Garden Court over grapefruit with her parents, Ann said, "You'll never believe this." They looked up. "I don't know how we could forget this," Ann said. "We forgot to get the marriage license!" Her parents stared at her. "So I'll have to go up to Sonoma County this morning. Ben can't do it without me."

"Okay," her mother said.

For a moment Ann felt a horror that her mother could believe that either she or Ben was that dumb. Then she was flooded with happiness that her mother was willing to accept her at her word.

But soon she was driving over the Bay Bridge towards the Oakland Courthouse thinking that while she was actually doing this, it would be for the last time, and soon she would be freed of this lying forever. She was reminded, as she drove, that the way the girders came forward and shot past overhead looked the way it would look if she were falling down some impossibly tall skyscraper. At least that's how it would be if she let herself really look at the girders.

Now inside the courthouse she had to pretend she was Elizabeth, for why else were they going to give her this award? She was playing a part in the house of the law in front of a clerk!

But soon she was speeding north on 101, crossing yet another bridge into deep blue and gold and she was free! Free! And she was going towards Ben! Towards her life in the country where she could do anything she pleased without hurting anyone's feelings. Shouldn't, indeed, her marriage make her parents a little bit happy? They were not the sort of people who wanted an unpopular daughter.

The hills started to undulate, shimmering gold. How Ann loved the feeling of space and eternity in the country! It made her remember Yosemite and other moments of being with nature from her childhood. There were animals on each side of the road.

Because they made doo doo, Ann's parents did not allow her to have any real pets when she was a child. Sure, both she and Barbara had turtles, but these soon dried up while racing. Then all that was left was a tropical island and a plastic palm tree. Then she and Barbara were each given a duckling. Ann's duckling started to grow and kept getting bigger. Everyone laughed at Ann's duck because it was so big. One morning, Ann got up and went out to her duck and it was no longer there! Her parents had taken both ducks away while she and her sister were still sleeping, had taken them away without asking to a lovely lake and let them go free because they made poop. At the park, another teeny tiny duck had come out of the water and shown the two city slickers how to swim. *And how happy all the ducks were!* Daddy said, while the tears rolled down Ann's cheeks. The tears were running down Ann's cheek now picturing for the first time the impossibly touching scene—her parents, younger than they were now, in the early morning light, driving together with two ducks in the car to a lake where they could swim off never to return.

After that, the only pets Ann had, besides a rabbit which developed a goiter and fungus on its back, had come from the experimental lab—one frog which never hopped and shrivelled up, followed by one that got more and more blubbery until finally it could bounce so high that it bounced over a hedge as tall as a house into a neighbor's yard and was never seen again. Actually, Ann realized as she drove, it was *Barbara* who went and got the pets from the experimental lab. Perhaps Ann had hallucinated some of this. This *was* about the same time that a dirigible came down into the back yard, a dirigible-shaped flying saucer came down and hovered over her, about two feet above where she could leap off the backyard fence with her arms reaching upwards.

But now that she was living in the country she could have any animal she wanted to have. One day Ann had come in from the pond and found a bunny in the basket next to the fireplace. This bunny had been left there by a thoughtful friend who had heard her speak pathetically of her childhood bunny. For some reason, Ann had decided to call this bunny Mrs. Rabbit. Ann built Mrs. Rabbit a hutch out of an old packing crate. She couldn't let her hop free—there were too many predators here—the red tailed hawk by day, by night the great horned owl. But every time Ann walked past the hutch where Mrs. Rabbit was she said to herself, "What kind of a life is this for a living being? She wants to go free!" Then, if it was at all possible, Ann would take Mrs. Rabbit out in the yard and let her graze on the green grass and hop about a bit. But not too much. Ann had to watch her to make sure her own dog didn't get her. How many minutes a day could she afford to give to this rabbit? And how many not to?

Here was her dog to greet her and to lead her home. Ann turned off the motor and the only sound was the wind in the trees. A naked man, dressed only in beard and moustache, with the pubic rhyme, was coming towards her along the path still wet from the pond. His skin was a dark pink-gold and his eyes a flash of blue. It was Ben!

"Come on," Ann said. "We should be getting to the courthouse."

"Don't you want to take a look at the garden first?" Ben asked.

"But we haven't got that much time," Ann said, following him into the garden. The wind was just getting up. But Ben had constructed a wind-screen at the end by the corn so that if you sat or lay on the blanket you would be in a still place with the weather of the earth rushing by overhead.

Printed February 1979 in Santa Barbara & Ann Arbor for the Black Sparrow Press by Mackintosh and Young & Edwards Brothers Inc. Design by Barbara Martin. This edition is published in paper wrappers; there are 200 hardcover copies numbered & signed by the author; & 26 lettered copies have been handbound in boards by Earle Gray, each with an original drawing by Sherril Jaffe.

Sherril Jaffe was born in 1945 in Walla Walla, Washington. When she was three, a doctor advised her parents never to allow her to learn to read or write because of her eyes. They were to move to the country so that she would not be tempted to go to school. At that time they were living in Los Angeles, close to the Tar-pits. It was here by the Tar-pits that she first developed a taste for the pastoral life. Nonetheless, eight years later the family moved to Beverly Hills where "the schools were better."

Later, at the Sorbonne, Ms. Jaffe would come to be known as "La Petite Choo-choo of the art department." But at age seventeen she left for New York and the Bowery, and the next year was arrested in a foreign country. When released, she remained on the Continent and studied with a noted hyphenated name at Le Havre, not far from Rouen. In 1968 she returned to California to prove her thesis.

Eventually, however, she did move to the country, where she wrote her first book, *Scars Make Your Body More Interesting*. She now lives on the outskirts of Sebastopol, where the flower always comes before the fruit.